What Has Triathlon Ever Done for Me?

Life Lessons From An Amateur Triathlete

Pete Eggleston

Contents

Dedication

For Luce

Thank you for everything

"The shit that makes your heart beat faster and your eyes glow when you do it or talk about it, no matter if it's hiking, yoga, gardening, painting, sex, meditation, photography, going for walks, helping others – do that. Do it as often as you can. Because that's what life is about. Creating as many passionate, happy moments as possible. Don't let anyone stop you from doing the things you love – not even yourself."

Introduction

Contrary to all expectations and dreams, I found myself running along a boiling hot sidewalk in the western Canadian town of Penticton in August 2017, saying to Lucy, my wife, 'Oh my God, I'm winning my age group in the world championships.' Luce's reply will always remain with me, keeping me grounded and entertained, 'not for long' as a very fast-running American chap was bearing down on me, rapidly eating into my relatively slender lead.

I ended up coming second in my age group that day, narrowly holding off some very rapid Canadians behind me, but it was a very special day. I don't remember any disappointment from achieving the 'first loser' spot, which will prove to be a useful trait in the future, given my preponderance for silver. Only four months previously I'd been told by a respiratory consultant that I wouldn't be training properly again for twelve months as I'd been hit by 'the biological equivalent of a bus'.

Triathlon has provided me with many incredibly special memories and experiences, and I'm very grateful that I have been able to pursue my passion for over twenty years. There are numerous triathlon books out there already describing various individuals and their journey, so why have I decided to wade in and start blethering away in prose? I think it is largely for my own benefit, so when I'm even older I will have a record that will remind me as I expect I'll be forgetting most of it.

I'm under no illusion that such a self-indulgent exercise is going to be of any interest to anyone else. I'm also aware that there may be other, much more successful, age group triathletes who come across this and think who the hell does he think he is?

Furthermore, there are also many in the triathlon world who look down their nose at the whole age group racing thing, amateurs who run around in their GB kit at weekends thinking they are the big I am, but this collection of thoughts isn't intended for them. There are always going to be haters, and especially in these times of polarising social media and keyboard warriors.

If you are one of those people and stumble across this, please just don't bother reading any of it. From a practical perspective, I'd like to write a novel one day and I remember hearing that to start writing, you should write about a subject that is familiar to you. Hence, kicking off with some witterings about triathlon will hopefully provide some writing practice for the future.

I have learnt many lessons along the way, and I will attempt to summarise those as I go. These aren't necessarily lessons about triathlon training and racing but are often more general lessons that apply to all aspects of life. There are many famous quotes and mantras I've come across over the years, but one of them applies at this point in the writing process (as it has done in many races), and that is from Maverick, aka Captain Pete Mitchell from Top Gun. Don't think, just do.

The Beginning

I have no sporting background. Certainly no background in endurance sports or any technical skills for swimming. Neither of my parents was sporty, although they were active. My brother and I spent many hours moaning as we were dragged on hikes around the UK throughout our childhood. I used to dread cross country during the winter term and dreaded athletics in the summer term even more.

I enjoyed team sports and played football, cricket, rugby and basketball at various points throughout secondary school, but I was mediocre at all of them. Not quite at the level of being the kid that got picked last, and enjoyed some success at rugby and cricket, but still pretty average. Indeed, the pinnacle of my childhood sporting endeavours was attending the Dorset U16 county rugby trials. I failed to be picked for the county team by a large margin.

I didn't learn to swim until I was 10. My first junior school in Sheffield didn't have a pool and we used to sometimes visit a local municipal pool, but I couldn't swim a width and found the whole experience decidedly traumatic. In 1978, when I was 9, we moved to the south coast, to a small town called Highcliffe, where the local junior school had a small pool.

With more opportunities to get in the water, I finally learnt to swim a width of 12.5m, breaststroke, without inhaling too much water. My distant memory of this was that I, together with my friend Darren, who I'm still in touch with, were the last members of the class to learn how to swim and were almost certainly ridiculed for it accordingly.

I remember this feeling like a very significant achievement at the time, although it was already very clear to me that my future was not going to involve swimming galas and championships. This didn't trouble me. I was a fairly weird, introverted kid who largely enjoyed his own company.

After leaving university and starting work, I probably slipped into what is a common pattern of limited exercise, a fair bit of socialising and drinking and consequential weight gain. I didn't ever get really overweight, but I do remember noticing the weight going up and generally not feeling great. We moved to Hong Kong for a couple of years in 1996, and although the socialising and drinking probably went up, we were lucky enough to live in an apartment that had a lovely pool.

For reasons that I now can't remember I decided to try to teach myself to swim a length of front crawl. Bear in mind this was in the days before you could just look up videos on YouTube or Instagram for tuition, so it was a lengthy process of trial and error, with lots of water swallowed along the way.

Eventually, at some point during 1997, I managed to achieve the goal of one length of front crawl and felt pretty chuffed with myself. I have no idea how long the length took me but I would guess it was very unimpressive. However, another life change would result in swimming getting forgotten about for some time.

At the beginning of 1998, we moved to Amsterdam as I was starting a different job. We arrived on New Year's Day, on a wet, windy, cold and dreary evening and promptly wished we were back in Asia. No fancy apartment with a pool here, just lots of rain, wind, sour milk and, thankfully, krentenbollen (a marvellous

Dutch delicacy that is basically a currant bun). We ended up buying an apartment and living in Amsterdam for over 4 years, and loving it, but it was a major culture shock after living in Hong Kong and took some getting used to.

Work was busy, especially whilst trying to get established in a new job in a new organisation, where I wasn't particularly welcomed by a new team. I was responsible for a risk management team within the Amsterdam dealing room of the bank ABN AMRO, and my new team members weren't too pleased about some random English bloke coming in. Looking back, they made it clear that they thought their Dutch colleague should have been put in charge of the team, making the atmosphere frosty at times.

The frostiness culminated one particular day a few months in when one of the team members decided it was time to let me know what she really thought of me. I can't remember the exact sequence of events that resulted in the explosion, and I'm pretty sure it was nothing too significant, but my colleague obviously felt differently, standing up from her desk in the middle of a large dealing room, screaming at me in Dutch, kicking her cabinet and storming off.

Lucy and I had started Dutch lessons, but my linguistic skills weren't yet at a level where I fully understood every word of the tirade of abuse, other than being called the c-word, which is remarkably similar in Dutch and English. The few minutes afterwards were the quietest I've ever heard in a dealing room in my almost 30-year career in financial markets.

Anyway, I digress, but suffice to say, I had my hands full at work and trying to maintain my momentum in swimming was far from my mind. However, the weight wasn't shifting and probably increasing, in no small part due to our new location with its fantastic social life, range of beers and culinary delights.

The previously mentioned delicacy krentenbollen is just one member of a large array of Dutch bollen, or ball-shaped, goodies that extended to oliebollen, bitterbollen and various others. I am a sucker for a bun and have no willpower, so this smorgasbord of bollen wasn't helping. I had to do something if I wanted to avoid becoming an overweight man in my middle age, and it had to be something that was easy to fit in around a busy work and life. Running. I started to run.

Initially, I thought running was great. I didn't find it easy and it was slow and lumbering, but I enjoyed the process of running. The time outside in the fresh air, with just my thoughts for company, was therapeutic and helped me destress. I wasn't too bothered about pace or distance and just ran from the front door, often around the Vondelpark in Amsterdam South, and simply enjoyed it for what it was.

I don't know how long this phase lasted but my running started to evolve to wanting to become quicker. A laudable goal for most people, but when you're just a bit dense and uneducated about training, this next phase wasn't a great outcome at first. I became a classic male, trying to push himself without too much structure, progression, recovery, warm-ups or anything that I now know is required.

The outcome was achilles injuries, which plagued me for some time and resulted in enormous frustration as the cycles of running and feeling like I was improving would then be cut short as another achilles flared up. Stupidly running through issues obviously resulted in the injuries getting worse, as did not getting any expert diagnosis or treatment.

My first race was a 10-mile run, 'Dam to Dam,' which was probably sometime around 1999 or 2000. I don't recall the time I managed but I do remember enjoying the experience of attending a mass event and participating in an actual race. I obviously wasn't in any way competitive and it was just about finishing, but looking back, this is probably when some competitive seeds were sown.

We returned to the UK in late 2001 and moved to St Albans, near where we lived prior to moving to Hong Kong. I was continuing to run, during the brief moments when not suffering from inflamed achilles tendons, and started to think a bit bigger, or should I say longer.

Such scope creep is common, but in 2002 I decided I wanted to run the London marathon and entered the 2003 race, running for 'Save the Rhino'. After meeting the charity and feeling the weight of the rhino costumes, I politely declined the fancy dress option and decided to run as an unencumbered human.

I was at least wise enough to recognise that a marathon was a significant undertaking and decided I needed to take things a little more seriously. By 2002, it was now possible to search this new-fangled internet thing for training plans and I settled on a plan I found by Hal Higdon. I have no idea why. It just sounded achievable.

Armed with a plan, my first structured training began, building up to 4-5 runs per week. The classic weekend long run gradually lengthened, although I think the longest run prior to the race was only 19 miles. I can still vaguely remember this particular run as I felt pretty broken by the end of it, although that may be due to the route I chose rather than the exertion.

Running to Luton and back wasn't the most inspiring route and dragging myself home that day felt like torture and I definitely recall thinking that I'd probably bitten off more than I could chew with a marathon.

Race day came in April 2003 and I loved it. Running the London marathon is one of the most memorable things I've ever done. You see London at its best, with so many people on the streets creating a unique atmosphere of positivity and happiness. It really is a very special day. I was thrilled to finish, although the last 8 miles or so were very painful.

One of my most vivid memories of the day was entering the Blackfriars tunnel and it looked like a scene from a war zone. Runners sitting on the kerb with their heads in their hands, others lying on their backs, others trying to stretch out various cramps. I'm quite certain I was walking at this point, but I wanted to make sure I finished.

With the beauty of hindsight gained over 20 years of subsequent endurance training, I can now see how the lack of conditioning resulted in a mediocre marathon debut, finishing in 4 hours and 26 minutes. But it didn't matter. I loved it, and unbeknown to me, at the finish line, I would be back.

So, we finally get to triathlon. I have no memory now of why I thought that I wanted to try a triathlon. I don't even know how I came across it as a sport. I wasn't one of these triathletes that you hear so often say that they remember watching the Kona World

Championships on TransWorld Sports on Saturday mornings on Channel 4 and thinking, 'One day, I want to go there.'

Nope, never heard of Kona. The only moment I can remember is saying to Lucy on New Year's Day in 2004 that one day I think I'd like to try a triathlon. It probably wasn't, but in what felt like minutes, she had entered me into the London Olympic distance triathlon that August. There you go, then.

Yikes. I had no idea what was involved, how to train, what kit I would need or indeed anything at all. One of the best early decisions I took was to join the local triathlon club in St Albans, Tri-Force, who were very welcoming and helpful. The club had around 50 members or so, with some very experienced and talented athletes (who seemed like complete triathlon Gods to me) and some complete newbies like me.

I needed a bike. Other than riding a tricycle and then a Grifter, as a kid, my cycling experience was effectively zero. When living in Amsterdam, we had bought bikes, and I sometimes rode to work, although we mostly used them to cycle around town, to the supermarket, back from the pub etc. This was always a challenge as coming home drunk whilst trying to avoid various obstacles, the most dangerous of which were tram tracks, as our friend Dan discovered, should have been good training for developing bike handling skills. Not in my case, as bike handling is still a weakness today, but at least I had a hybrid bike, which we'd brought back from Amsterdam.

Bike training didn't start particularly well. Not having a turbo trainer at this point, training basically involved getting out on my hybrid bike and tootling around St Albans and the surrounding area. One weekday morning before work, I was coming to the end of a ride, heading back into St Albans, and approaching a T-junction somewhere near Sandridge.

I could see a large Mercedes sitting at the T-junction, waiting to pull out and turn right across me. It was my right of way and I distinctly remember catching the eye of the driver, at which point I stupidly assumed that he had seen me and would wait for me to go by before pulling out. How foolish of me.

As I came up alongside the junction, the Mercedes simply pulled out right in front of me, causing me to go over its bonnet and land in a heap in the middle of the road. The next memory I have is coming round in the back of an ambulance.

Luckily, I wasn't badly hurt. Some bruises and road rash, but nothing was broken. I remember calling Luce, who was at work already and said there was nothing to worry about. I was in an ambulance after getting hit by a car, but all was ok and I'd be going to the hospital to get checked over. I suggested there was no need to come to the hospital, which was greeted with a 'Don't be stupid, of course, I'm coming.' En route to Watford General the paramedic in the back of the ambulance showed me my bike helmet, which was destroyed. He calmly said that if I hadn't been wearing it, I would now have, at best, a very serious head injury or, at worst, be dead. Those words stayed with me and I've always worn a helmet ever since. Life can be turned upside down in seconds and I was very aware of how lucky I had been.

Some time later, I retrieved my bike, which a kind passerby who lived close to the accident had taken in. The bike was surprisingly ok, which was a shame really, as it would have been a perfect excuse to buy a new bike[1], so I decided to get back on as quickly as possible, although I retain an over-cautiousness to this day when cycling by any car waiting to pull out in front of me.

Apart from getting flattened by a Mercedes, I was enjoying the training. The variety was good and contributed to my staying injury-free, for now at least.

Swimming was a challenge, and I attended the club swims every Monday evening to try to get some advice and technique development from the two Tri-Force swim coaches. I was very firmly rooted in the slow lane and progress seemed incredibly slow. I quickly figured out that swimming was very unlike biking and running, where you just needed to put the work in and you would improve. Swimming was a whole different kettle of fish and something I would struggle with for the next 20 years.

Tri-Force put on a number of races throughout the season, the first of which was a pool-based sprint triathlon at Hatfield Leisure Centre. I decided that it would be a good idea to do this race before standing on the start line at the London Triathlon in August. I bought a tri-suit and researched what to do regarding transitions. I didn't have cleats on my hybrid bike, so I would be riding in running shoes. The days of attaching bike shoes to my pedals and flying dismounts were a long way in the future.

Race day dawned on April 25[th,] 2004. I can't remember the race that well, but luckily, I have recorded details of every race and training session I've done so I can recall how it went.

The 400m swim seemed to go on forever, although I exited the

---

[1] Nowadays I find that no such excuse is required

water at 8:45 and headed off into transition to find my bike. I do remember feeling pretty embarrassed by my hybrid sit-up and beg bike racked in transition alongside very impressive-looking road and triathlon bikes, but I didn't spend any time dwelling on it, hopped on and headed off on the 20km course.

I did get lost, taking a wrong turn at a roundabout, and was furious with myself as I pedalled back into transition. The bike took 46:43 at an average of just over 17mph. No bike shoes obviously resulted in a relatively speedy T2, and I was off on what I thought was my strength, given my running pedigree[2].

The 5k was a flat 2-lap route, and I finished it in 26 mins, with a total time of 1 hour and 24 mins. But it didn't matter. I loved the whole experience and was totally and utterly hooked. The triathlon bug had well and truly bitten.

Training over the next few months increased. Looking at my training log for 2004, I can see I was averaging around 4-5 hours per week in the first few months of the year, but this gradually increased over the period May to July, peaking at just over 8 hours in mid-July. There was little structure other than the weekly club swim, although I was practising running off the bike.

Other than that I can see that each bike and run session was basically 'go out and go as quickly as you can for whatever the planned duration is'. The first recorded interval session, other than some random fartlek run sessions, was a bike session in June. How things have changed. However, I can see that I was getting quicker, with the bike improvements seemingly developing the fastest, and

---

[2] This is sarcastic

I was looking forward to the London event, scheduled for August 1st.

I'd entered the Olympic, or standard, distance event, which comprised of a 1500m swim, 40km bike and 10km run. It would be my first attempt at this distance and I was nervous, compounded by the fact that the event was on a scale I hadn't experienced before. Held at the Excel Centre in East London, the swim was in a dock near to City airport.

My abiding memory of the swim was the taste of jet fuel in the water, and I felt the customary relief upon exiting the water and running up the stairs into the transition in Excel. The swim had taken 31:15, which was faster than the sprint event in April, although the majority of that improvement was probably due to the wetsuit[3].

The bike leg was fantastic. I had now binned the hybrid and bought my first ever road bike, a Giant OCR, which I loved. The course headed west, through the Limehouse tunnel, down the Embankment and turned around at Westminster. It was great fun. The bike leg took just under 70 minutes, averaging just over 21mph, and represented a big personal best for me at the time for 40km.

On to the run, which I think was a fair chunk short of 10km[4], as I finished in 38:56, which represented a huge 10k PB for me. The overall time was 2:26:19, which surpassed my wildest

---

[3] To this day I am still considerably faster in a wetsuit than without, resulting in the classic anxious wait for water temperatures to be confirmed in the lead up to races

[4] I didn't have anything like a GPS watch at this point so have no idea of the exact distance

expectations, although I have no recollection now of what those expectations were. The experience had fuelled my love for the sport and I was keen to see how I could develop further.

2004's 'season' brought two more races, the Bedford Olympic race at the end of August and the Tri-Force club championships, a sprint race in September. Nothing notable to record from these races, although the improvements continued and I remained hooked.

Lucy and I have chatted on a number of occasions over the years, trying to figure out why the triathlon bug took hold so quickly and firmly. It clearly wasn't going to be a fad. Our most likely theory is simply the timing. We had been trying for a family for a number of years, moving back to the UK at the end of 2001 to embark upon three cycles of IVF.

None of these were successful and at the end of 2002, we made the very difficult decision to stop trying. We discussed adoption at length and decided that it was not for us, and we started to try to come to terms with the realisation that we were not going to be parents. This was not easy

With no family to care for and provide for, you do start to ask yourself, 'What is the point of me,' and how am I going to spend my time? I'm well aware that some folk who have become parents may well be saying at this point, oh, poor you, you've got so much time on your hands and you don't know what to do. What a first-world problem. And yes, maybe it is a first-world problem, but until you are in that situation, do not underestimate how it turns your world upside down.

I think finding triathlon was, in some ways, an escape from the grieving, albeit a temporary and, at times, an ineffectual escape.

Putting the navel-gazing to one side, whatever the reason, triathlon did provide me with something I was clearly looking for or needing, possibly subconsciously.

Lesson learnt: you don't need to be a child prodigy to either enjoy or be relatively successful at anything you put your mind to.

Although 2004's race results weren't necessarily a predictor of the relative age group success to come, I have come to realise that my lack of sporting childhood hasn't hindered my enjoyment of the sport.

Yes, if I had learnt to swim properly as a kid, I would be a better triathlete today, but I've worked hard at this and also focused on areas where I can try to compensate for the relatively weak swim, for example, the bike.

Belief

When did I start to believe that I could be half decent, for my age, at triathlon? It took a fair few more years for that belief to start to develop. I now realise just how important the mental side of training and racing is and that, without proper focus, it can have a very negative effect.

With the first triathlon 'season' completed, the desire to improve and carry on training and racing only increased. I stayed with sprint and Olympic distance races in 2005 and 2006, with no particular standout performance. One memory that sticks out is kicking off 2005 by racing the Blenheim sprint tri, which was a fantastic setting and the first race that my parents came to watch.

Again, nothing special in terms of performance, but I do remember really enjoying it, apart from almost chucking up on the very steep run up from the swim into transition. I also raced the Windsor, Milton Keynes and Bedford Olympic distance races in 2005, together with the club championships, knocking a full 1 second off my time from the previous year. My triathlon progress was glacial at this stage, although with the gift of hindsight, it is no huge surprise. Training volumes remained relatively low, and there was little structure or plan.

In terms of races, 2006 was almost a copy of 2005, with return visits to Windsor, Milton Keynes and Bedford. However, the glacial pace of improvement had increased, knocking off, for example, just over 20 minutes from my time at Milton Keynes compared to the previous year. This set my personal best for an Olympic distance race, at 2 hours 17 minutes, and getting faster was becoming addictive.

I was still racing on a road bike and continued to swim like a house brick, but the bike and run performances were getting better as the volume increased a little further and I learnt more about the process and physiology of training for endurance sports. The 2006 season again ended with the club championship sprint race, where I bettered my previous year's 1-second gain, coming in almost 3 minutes faster.

I think it was at some point in 2006 that I heard about the age group structure for racing internationally and representing your country. Tri-Force had a few members who had represented Great Britain, who I looked up to at the time as complete triathlon gods. Representing your country seemed like such an incredibly cool and prestigious goal to aim for, and I started to look into how you went about trying to achieve it over the winter of 2006.

After some surfing of the British Triathlon website, I figured out that for the World Championships, you needed to place highly in your age group at one of 3 or 4 qualifying races. The European Championships, at the time, were different in that you simply had to submit your best Olympic distance time in the previous year and places were allocated on a discretionary basis.

Each age group had 20 qualifying slots. I decided to give it a go for the 2007 season, entering the Shropshire, Dambuster, Northampton and Bala qualifying races. It was time to take this triathlon lark a bit more seriously and I threw myself into the winter training with significant enthusiasm.

After a winter and spring, where the training volume increased by approximately a third compared to the previous year[5], I was eagerly anticipating the 2007 season. The first race was the Shropshire Olympic distance race on June 10th, and unbeknown to me at the time, it attracted a very strong field given it was the first qualifying race of the year. I figured out later that all the fast folks like to qualify early on and that to qualify, in those days at least, you really needed to be smart and tactical about your race choices.

I was nervous that morning. More nervous than any other race so far. Racking my trusty road bike in transition that morning did nothing to alleviate my imposter syndrome as I watched all these racing snakes ooze confidence with their very impressive-looking TT bikes. Luce was a rock, as always, helping to calm me down as I headed off to the race start.

I ended up delivering a decent performance, setting a new PB, and finishing in 2 hours 11 minutes. The 40km bike leg time of 65 minutes and the 10km run time of just over 38 minutes were both the fastest I'd achieved to date, and I was stoked. Until I checked out the results later, I had come 23rd in the 35-39 age group. 23rd! There were 4 qualifying slots available for the 2008 World Championships, to be held in Vancouver the following June.

It was the biggest wake up call I can recall in all my years of triathlon. I was so far away from achieving this goal of representing my country and I was utterly humbled. It felt like a long drive home down the M6 and M1 that evening. Far from developing any belief, this experience had provided the exact

---

[5] My 2007 training log indicates I averaged just over 8.5 hours per week of total training

opposite.

There was little time to pull myself together. The next qualifier, Dambuster, was in 2 weeks time. I have come to realise that I do possess some resilience and dogged determination, so I put Shropshire behind me, focusing on the positives of the performance and prepared as best I could for Dambuster on June 23rd.

Dambuster proved to be even more humbling. Another decent performance gave me 24th in my age group. Checking out the results, I was once again humbled to see that the winner of my age group was almost exactly 10 minutes faster than I was, which seemed like an enormous gulf at that time over an Olympic distance race. Looking back over the results, it is interesting to see many of the names that raced that day still competing today.

I had one last chance that year; the last qualifier of the year was in North Wales at Bala. My parents lived in North Wales at this point, so I decided to couple the race with a visit to see them. I raced Northampton Olympic the week before, on September 9th, as a warm-up after a break from racing during July and August.

The race went well, setting a new PB at this distance with a 2hr 10min finish time, but still only finishing 15th in my age group. Race week for Bala was a mixture of emotions. On one hand, I knew I was improving, but I was also aware that I was still some away from the pointy end of my age group.

We travelled up to Wales on Saturday, met my parents in Bala and did a recce of the bike course with Luce and my Dad. I loved the course, some climbing but also some very quick sections, even on a road bike.

Back then, for the Bala event, the roads would be completely closed on race day as well, a feature that has sadly become unusual for UK triathlons nowadays. I was excited and nervous, determined to end the season with a performance where I gave it everything.

I now can't remember why, but the swim was shortened on race morning to 1000m, I think due to high winds and cold temperatures. Given my weak swim, this should play to my strengths, so I wasn't too upset with the decision. I managed to survive the swim and had a decent bike split of just over an hour. I had no idea where I was in the race but I thought I was going well given how many people I'd overtaken. The run was a bit lumpy and I buried myself, finishing in 2hrs and 5mins.

Looking back now, I do remember mixed emotions at the finish. I was pleased with my performance but was also very disappointed to only finish 10th in my age group, well outside the top 4 automatic qualifying spots. I obviously wasn't aware how many people ahead of me were either trying to qualify or had already qualified (this analysis would come later when the full results were published – yes, kids, back in 2007, there wasn't real-time online tracking!). However, I seriously doubted that the qualification roll-down would make it to the 10th spot. Another long drive home down the M6 and M1 beckoned whilst I ruminated on my 2007 season.

Work was particularly busy at this point in my life, and I was travelling a lot. This proved to be a healthy distraction from the triathlon, and I pushed it to the back of my mind for a few weeks. In the autumn of 2007, I had a long business trip to Asia, travelling to Hong Kong, Singapore, Tokyo and Seoul.

I particularly remember this trip due to the phone call I had from my hotel room in Seoul one evening. I had received a message that someone from British Triathlon was trying to contact me at home. Somewhat confused, I called them back and was greeted with the news that my Bala result had proved to be enough to be offered a roll-down slot for the world championships in Vancouver next June. Back then, British Triathlon called around the individuals on the roll-down list, offering them the slot before moving on down the list. I happily and gratefully accepted the slot, putting the phone down in a slight state of shock, before celebrating by ordering room service and calling Luce to tell her the news.

The feeling of satisfaction was enormous. I had set myself a goal, worked hard, learnt from setbacks along the way and managed to achieve something I would never have dreamt of as a child running around at the back of a cold, wet, muddy cross-country run at school. The satisfaction was tinged with a sense of imposter syndrome in that it was a roll-down qualification slot and not an automatic slot.

From listening to age groupers on podcasts and reading blogs over the years, I think imposter syndrome is pretty common and it felt uncomfortable. I decided to use it to fuel the fire for training over the winter and quickly set my goal for Vancouver, which was to ensure I wasn't the last GB athlete in my age group!

The winter of 2007-2008 is when I feel that my triathlon training and subsequent performances underwent a step change. My training became much more structured, focused and progressive, largely based on material I was reading and through advice from club members.

I particularly remember working very hard on the turbo during the winter, banging out weeks of hard interval sessions. This was motivated by the goal of not coming last and trying to prove to myself that I was racing for my country on merit. This goal had come forward a little as I had discovered that the 2008 European championships would be in Lisbon in May, and at that point, there weren't qualification races for the Europeans.

You had to submit your best Olympic race result from the previous year, and the team manager allocated slots on a discretionary basis. I submitted my result from Bala and was delighted to get a slot. Other than a local sprint, this race in Lisbon would be the first race of the 2008 season and would prove to be a turning point.

In addition to the changes in training, I also acquired my first time trial bike in early 2008. The company I worked for, RBS, had decided to sponsor me once they'd heard about the qualification for the world champs, and this sponsorship came in the form of a new bike. Acquired from our local bike shop in St Albans, Addiktion Cycles, I was now the proud owner of a Trek TTX triathlon bike.

I fell in love immediately. It took some time to get used to the very different riding position, but gradually I became more and more comfortable riding in the aero position and was also very happy to find that running off the bike felt better. We ordered the GB tri suit, and this arriving in the post was the icing on the excitement cake. Motivation and anticipation were high as the season approached.

We travelled to Lisbon with friends Darren and Mary and planned to have a few days enjoying somewhere we hadn't been before. This has proven to be a theme in the ensuing years as triathlon has taken us to many places around the world, most of which we probably wouldn't have ever visited otherwise.

As newbies, we decided to stay in the team hotel (something we would try to avoid in subsequent trips to avoid anxious triathletes) and enjoyed the build-up to race day. My recollection is a little blurry now around the event, but one standout memory is the talk given by the team manager, Scott Murray, on the evening prior to the race. He was inspirational and passionate, telling us to simply go out there and be great, racing with pride. I was pretty fired up!

Race day dawned. I had no expectations, and other than hoping I wouldn't come last, I just wanted to enjoy the experience. The swim was in a dock and I came out of the water well down the field of over 80 athletes in the 40-44 age group at 23:48.

My day would get better as I headed out onto the bike, which was a pretty uninspiring course up and down a dual carriageway. The rain had started to come down, but I got my head down and started picking off athletes. It was my first experience of international racing and I was shocked at the blatant drafting on the bike, something that would wind me up to this day. However, I had a great day on the new bike, delivering the fastest bike split of my age group, and headed off on the run. A 10k PB of just over 37 minutes resulted in me finishing 7th in my age group and the first GB athlete, a result I was absolutely flabbergasted with. I was also only 90 seconds away from the podium, which would prove to be a significant motivator for the future.

Total shock. I knew that my winter training had gone well, but I had no idea that this level of performance was remotely possible. Sitting in the bar that evening, celebrating with Luce, Darren and

Mary, I can safely say that imposter syndrome was the last thing on my mind. To answer my question at the beginning of the chapter, it was May 11th, 2008, in Lisbon that I finally started to believe.

Lesson: hard, consistent work pays off.

With no natural talent or helpful sporting background, my only option was to work hard, but I definitely learnt over this period that if you set yourself a goal, devise a realistic plan, and deliver on that plan, then dreams can come true. When this happens, you start to believe in yourself.

Values

Lisbon moved the goalposts. I was no longer focused on not coming last or embarrassing myself. The goal of trying to qualify to race for my country only 12 months ago had now morphed into, one day, trying to get on an international age group podium. Given that I hadn't managed to do this domestically reinforced just how much of a stretch goal this was, although those 90 seconds in Lisbon seemed to tempt me into at least trying. It would take many more years to achieve this goal and a key lesson I would learn on the way was that I wouldn't be able to do it on my own.

Back to 2008 and the World Championships in Vancouver. We planned a decent holiday around the trip, the first part of which we were going to share with our friends Dan and Kate. Unfortunately, Vancouver experienced particularly unusual weather that June, with very low temperatures, high winds and more rain than usual.

This disrupted some of our holiday plans, for example, cancelled seaplane flights getting replaced with a transfer via a stretch limo, but also affected race day. I'd been for a practice swim a couple of days before the race, and the water was incredibly rough and cold. The weather still hadn't improved by race day and the organisers cancelled the swim, turning the race into a duathlon by replacing the swim with a 5k run. Ironically, for someone who was a weaker swimmer, I discovered that day that I really didn't enjoy duathlons.

I've had a few laboratory fitness tests done over the years, largely to accurately find threshold levels and determine substrate consumption at different intensity levels. All of these tests have confirmed that I am fundamentally a diesel engine with little if any, top end. If it were possible, I think I could count the number of fast twitch fibres in my body on one hand. I take a long time to warm up and have discovered over the years that triathlon suits me as the swim allows my body to 'get going' and gradually increase my HR (not having any swim speed, I find it difficult getting my HR into three figures whilst swimming), unlike a 5k run at the beginning of a duathlon. This proved to be far too much of a shock to the diesel, and I was well and truly blowing out of my arse within minutes of the gun going off. I had a newfound respect for duathletes.

The bike course was relatively technical around Stanley Park, and I learnt another lesson. I needed to improve my bike handling skills as I underperformed relative to blatting up and down a dual carriageway in Lisbon. The final run was pretty decent, clocking another sub-38-minute 10k. I ended up coming 25th and the 7th GB athlete (out of 20), so my original goal was achieved, and I felt like I had justified my roll-down slot.

The 2008 season went well once returning from Canada. In early July, I raced my first National Championships at Wakefield and surprised myself with a first age group podium and a silver medal. Back to the old favourite Milton Keynes Olympic distance later in July resulted in another second place in the age group and a new PB over the distance, now getting frustratingly close to breaking 2 hours.

The highlight of domestic racing in 2008 came in August, back at the London Triathlon, where this had all begun. My wave was the first of the morning, and after a usual average swim, I quickly worked my way into the lead on the bike in the first few miles.

This meant I was the first rider headed down Embankment towards Westminster, with police motorbikes around me to ensure traffic control. I will always remember this experience. It was magical, hammering through Blackfriars tunnel and down a deserted Embankment. I'm not sure if it was due to excitement, adrenaline, or the exertion level, but it was the first time I was sick in my mouth in a race, but even that doesn't detract from the memory! I won the 40-44 age group that day, the first time on the top step, and it felt great doing it back at the race where I first discovered my love for the sport.

Why was 2008 so different to 2007? I was nowhere near getting on the podium in my age group the previous year and the guys that were felt like they were on a totally different level. I had moved up to 40-44 from the 35-39 age group, although this probably wasn't a significant factor as the performance differences at this age were pretty small (unlike, as I would find later, than between say 50-54 and 55-59). Training volume increased, going from just over 8.5 hours per week in 2007 to 12 hours in 2008. But there were many other factors, including a much more structured and focused training plan. Moving from a road bike to a TT bike also made a tangible difference. Lastly, I think the mental side played a large part. The self-doubt had largely gone and I was starting to believe in myself, creating a virtuous feedback loop with each race result.

The season wrapped up with me dipping my toe in the world of longer-distance racing at the Vitruvian middle-distance race in September. I enjoyed it, finishing 5th in my age group in 4 hrs 21 minutes, which I was pleased with. More lessons were learnt this day, the most important of which related to nutrition. At this point I had absolutely no idea about how to fuel a longer distance race and hadn't practised in training.

So I happily tucked into solid fuel on the bike, including flapjacks and malt loaf, thinking all was good. How wrong I was. The run at Vitruvian goes around the reservoir and out across a dam, a section which is pretty exposed with little cover. This proved to be unfortunate as my malt loaf decided it needed an exit, and I experienced my first major gastrointestinal distress.

With no other options open to me, I had to crouch on the side of the path on the dam, unpeel my trisuit and go to the loo. With athletes running by at pretty close proximity, the embarrassment levels were high and I recall crouching there apologising in a very English way to everyone who went by, saying how terribly sorry I was. The humiliation stayed with me, and I didn't attempt solid food again in a race.

I finished the 2008 season very motivated and attacked winter training like a man possessed. The Olympic Distance World Champs were scheduled to be in Australia in 2009, on the Gold Coast in Queensland. Lucy and I hadn't spent time in Australia on holiday, so we started to plan a trip, dependent on me qualifying the following year. A trip of a lifetime certainly provided extra training motivation, not that anymore was really needed.

Outside of triathlon, life at work was changing fast. I had been studying part-time for an MSc in Biodiversity Conservation and Management at Imperial College with a view to exiting the world of finance at some point. The financial crisis of 2007-08 accelerated this career change to some extent as I became more and more disillusioned. I was still working for RBS as the head of a quantitative advisory team, which basically provided a service to investors around the world trying to help improve their investment returns through the provision of mathematical models and software.

During the period of hubris in financial markets leading up to the crisis, RBS, in their infinite wisdom, decided to embark upon a hostile takeover of the Dutch bank ABN AMRO. At the time, I think this was due to be the largest ever bank takeover and the ego of RBS's CEO, Fred Goodwin, was the main driving force in what would become a colossal mistake.

As a result of the takeover, many RBS employees, including myself, had to reapply for jobs in the newly merged organisation. I was tempted at this point, I think during 2007, to not bother and exit, but my pride probably stopped me as I was offended at having to reapply for my own job in the first place. Anyway, I was told my application for my own job was successful, so I tried to carry on, get my head down, and deliver for our clients. This didn't last too long as the previously mentioned hubris and ego surrounding me proved to be too much in the end.

Everything came to a head on one particular morning sometime in late 2008. The financial crisis was still in full swing, and it was clear that pure greed, arrogance and dishonesty contributed to the disaster that was now affecting the global economy. I was presenting to the global sales team that morning, providing an overview of one of the latest products that my team had developed. This product was an investment model where clients could follow the trading signals that the model systematically generated, thereby providing an investment return. We had tested the model historically, and the results showed it would have provided investors with something like a 7% annual return over the last 5 years or so (I can't remember the exact numbers).

The Global Head of Structured Product Sales (or some such ridiculous job title), a chap called Didier, was not impressed with these returns. He told me that our competitors were selling similar products that offered better returns and could I please just adjust or tweak our results to improve them.

I politely and patiently tried to explain that this was a purely quantitative framework, there was no subjective element involved, so the results were simply what they were. We could research some other approaches, but that would obviously take time. He repeated his request, this time in a much angrier and frustrated manner, and I again politely declined, asking him to confirm that he basically wanted me to lie? He pretty much spat at me that he did. The exchange became more heated, and although I can't remember all the exact details, I do remember the climax of the meeting.

Those who know me well know that I am generally a fairly calm and reasonable individual. However, when the red mist does finally descend, it tends to arrive with a bang, and Didier had pushed me over the threshold. I informed him that in my opinion, one of the main reasons that the global financial industry was embroiled in the worst crisis for generations was due to people like him.

People whose ego and sheer greed drove them to behave in unethical and immoral ways, regardless of the consequences, if it meant that they would get paid that bit more. Silence fell in the room and on the conference call lines (there were probably around 80-100 people present around the world). Didier sat back in his chair, huffing and puffing, and shouted at me. Did I know what the problem in this room was? The problem was that the average IQ in the room was too high. I hadn't expected this but did happily inform him that that was a problem I could actually help him with, and I stood up and walked out.

I walked straight from the conference room to the large corner office on the edge of the dealing room, inhabited by the global head of the financial markets business (not sure how many layers of management this was above my head, but I knew this guy and liked him), and announced I was leaving.

There were a few more twists and turns, and weeks of discussions that aren't worthy of writing any more paragraphs about, but the end result was that I took voluntary redundancy and left the financial industry in February 2009. I was apprehensive about what was to come next, but I wanted to try and do something that I felt was more worthwhile. But this apprehension was more than compensated for by the excitement of having more time to train.

I finished my MSc in 2009, concluding with a dissertation that researched optimal habitat for water voles. Whilst wandering around the local countryside looking for water vole poo, I also started volunteering with my local Wildlife Trust, which largely involved habitat management with a bunch of old guys and their dogs. It was great fun, although, after years of a desk job, I wasn't used to a day of physical activity and found myself getting very tired.

Over time, I learnt that I needed to make larger packed lunches, as they were invariably disappearing by about 10:30 am every day at the first coffee break.

With the career change in full swing, I managed to ramp the training up with the weekly volume growing to average between 14 and 15 hours. The season was due to kick off at the Grendon Sprint on 10th May, which was a qualifier for the Sprint World Champs. I didn't want to qualify as I had already figured out that the sprint distance wasn't my thing due to my lack of fast twitch fibres, but I was keen to test myself in a strong age group field. I came 2nd in my category and was pleased with the performance, particularly the run (a 17:11 was a 5k PB at the time).

Two weeks later came the first main race of the year, Little Beaver, the first Olympic Distance qualifier for the World Champs on the Gold Coast. Given it was the first qualifier, and the destination was Australia, it was due to be a stacked start list as everyone would want to get a slot early so they could plan the trip in plenty of time. We travelled up the day before to allow a bike course recce, which proved very useful as it was a pretty technical route with a few lumps and twisty sections.

The goal was simply to bag one of the first 4 automatic qualification slots so we could start planning our holiday, but the nerves were high on race morning. The weedy, shallow lake wasn't the best swim venue, and I gave up the customary 2-3 minutes to the fastest swimmers in my AG, but I was 5th coming into transition, which was a new experience for me. The increased swim focus over the last few months had paid off.

The bike course was slightly short of 40km, but I had a blast and clocked the only sub 1 hour time in the AG, putting me in 2nd place as I headed out on the run. The run was 3 lumpy laps around the grounds of Belvoir Castle, but I managed to take the lead before the 5km mark and held on for the 40-44 win. I was ecstatic. The qualification experience couldn't be more different to the previous one for Vancouver; no humiliation, no waiting for a roll-down slot, and no imposter syndrome. Mission well and truly accomplished at the first time of asking.

The next main race (I was doing the odd sprint at Dorney Lake to try to stay sharp) was the British Middle Distance National Champs, back at Bala Lake in North Wales. The momentum from Little Beaver continued as I secured my first national title, clocking 4:15 to finish 8th overall and 1st in the 40-44 AG. It was another great day on the bike, clocking the fastest split in the category and heading out on the hilly run in the lead. I still hadn't nailed my nutrition, even though I avoided malt loaf, and needed to stop on the run a couple of times for the loo.

Thankfully, the Bala course was much less exposed, with plenty of vegetation to hide in, so the embarrassment of Vitruvian wasn't repeated. Luckily, I had a decent lead, so I didn't panic and eased off to win by just under 7 minutes. With Mum and Dad living not far away, it was good to have them there to see the awards presentation, and we headed back on the long journey home much happier than the last time I raced at Bala.

Next up were the Olympic distance European Championships, this year held at Holten in the Netherlands. One of my best mates, Stu, and his wife, Emma, joined us for the Dutch leg of the trip, after spending a few days prior in the Ardennes with Luce's sister, Caroline, and boyfriend, BH. I went into Holten with high hopes, given my current form and my debut at Lisbon the previous year, although it proved to be a chastening experience. It was a very hot weather spell, and the swim was declared non-wetsuit early on, which I knew was going to put me at even more of a disadvantage from the gun. I was right, coming out of the water in over 26 minutes and giving up almost 6 minutes to the fastest swimmer in the age group[6]. I ended up coming 12th, which felt like a step backwards after the 7th at Lisbon, but it was a good lesson in not basing your view of the race on position.

The start list varies considerably and it was clear that Holten was a much stronger field, in conditions that didn't play to my strengths. We had a good holiday, and it was just a hobby, so I don't remember dwelling for too long on the relative disappointment. It did reiterate to me how my swim simply wasn't good enough, and the lack of a wetsuit highlighted this even further. Trying to improve as an adult onset swimmer would prove to be the most frustrating project on the triathlon journey.

Before heading off the Australia, I had a couple more Olympic distance races, returning to the Milton Keynes race and also racing in Hyde Park. I won my age group at both and was clearly still in decent form. The Milton Keynes race was particularly memorable as it was the first time I managed to get on the overall podium at a relatively large race, finishing 3rd behind Adam Bowden and Dan Corner. I also managed to get below 2 hrs for the first time, finishing in 1:57, albeit on the notoriously short MK course. I haven't ever been too hung up on personal bests in triathlon as courses are so varied in terms of terrain, but also measurement

---

[6] The fastest swimmer was Olaf Geserick, an extremely talented triathlete from Germany, who would become my nemesis at many European Championships in the future. I think Holten was my first encounter with Olaf, and it quickly became Olaf 1 Pete 0

accuracy. However, dipping under 2 hours for an Olympic distance race did feel like a key benchmark.

We headed off to Australia in early September, flying into Brisbane. The plan was to spend a week or so prior to the race on the Gold Coast, then head back to Brisbane, relax on the Great Barrier Reef for a few days and then pick up an RV and drive down the coast to Sydney. It really felt like trip of a lifetime stuff and we were excited for the adventure. Sadly, the race experience put me off racing GB Age Group for a few years.

Prior to the main event I decided to race the Aquathlon, given we had travelled all that way. The less said about that, the better and my lesson learnt was not to do another race which didn't involve a bike. It did help acclimatise to the conditions a little and I was excited to see what I could do. My goal was to place better than I had at Vancouver as I felt I was a much better triathlete, but Holten had taught me that who was on the start list was out of your control, so I tried to simply focus on delivering my best on the day.

I had a decent swim, 21:50, thanks to the wetsuit and salt water, and headed out to attack the bike course. The course was 2 laps, flat on long, straight roads, which should have suited me down to the ground. Coming to the first turn round, approximately 10km into the ride, I was disappointed and angry to see a large pack of my age group coming the other way.

There was no pretence of trying to avoid any drafting, they looked like the peloton in a Grand Tour. I was determined to ride legally but knew I wouldn't be able to compete with such large packs. On the 2nd lap, I could see that the gap had grown, but I was even more angry to see a technical official on a moped riding alongside one of the packs and not issuing a single penalty.

I was shouting and gesticulating from the other side of the road as I could recognise guys in the group (names on the kit is a bit of a giveaway), including a GB athlete in my age group, but it was pointless. I headed out on the run knowing I was some way back, but I gave it everything and was happy with a 38-minute 10k under what had become a very hot Australian sun and off what I knew was a legal bike leg.

I finished in 2:02, which gave me 23rd place. Although this was a marginal improvement in terms of place compared to the previous year, I felt flat and was outraged at the very blatant cheating. I have always had a strong sense of right and wrong and tend to get a tad riled at what I feel are injustices. This day was one of those days. Analysis of the results clearly showed the effect of the drafting with guys having much faster bike splits than I had, even though I had been beating them on the bike multiple times over the last two years. I still loved triathlon, the training and racing had already become a lifestyle, but I decided that day to give the GB team a miss, at least for a while, if it wasn't going to be possible to race fairly.

On the subject of values, I've seen a fair bit of cheating over the years, including lots of drafting and also cutting swim and run courses short. The other area, which I haven't actually witnessed but am aware happens, is doping in age group triathlon.

The fact that people take banned substances simply to place better in a triathlon, which is an amateur hobby, absolutely staggers me. It is widely reported how easy it is, for example, to acquire testosterone in some countries through the health system by simply playing the low libido card for middle-aged men. I have seen some bizarre results over the years, when men in their 50s, especially those who have been racing for some time, all of a sudden start producing results that are a step change from previous results. If you've been training and racing for many years, then it is highly suspicious if you continue to get faster into your late 50s, especially on the run.

My run times have been declining since 2013 when I set my PBs at almost all distances. Even though I'm training more than ever, my nutrition is better; I wear carbon-plated super shoes, do more strength training, and I'm sleeping more. Yes, I know, I'm an n=1 study, but I firmly believe that you are defying biology if your run times all of a sudden improve after 10-20 years of competing and you are in your 50s or older.

Needless to say, ethically, I wouldn't dream of taking a banned substance simply to try to win my age group in any race, never mind the potential negative long-term health implications of doing so. To those of you who are doing so, I pity you and don't understand how you can look at yourself in the mirror. Rant over.

Lesson: be true to yourself.

Work

Life changed significantly again in 2010. I had tried to find permanent work in the conservation sector following the completion of my MSc in 2009, but with little success. In the summer of 2009, I took an intern role at the conservation group of the Zoological Society of London (ZSL), working for Sarah Christie on the genetic breeding programme for Amur leopards and tigers. I really enjoyed the work and ignored the fact that I was the oldest intern, at 40, that ZSL had probably ever had.

However, there wasn't a permanent role available at the end of the internship. When we returned from Australia in October, I took a 6-month contract at the Herts & Middlesex Wildlife Trust, but again, at the end of the period, there wasn't a suitable permanent role. So, by the spring of 2010, I was out of work and decided to focus on training through the summer, ahead of what would be that year's A race, the iconic Alpe d'Huez triathlon.

This plan didn't kick off too well. In the spring, I returned to the London Marathon for the 3rd time and managed to pick up an achilles injury. My wiser, older self would have managed this injury much better, but I was a foolish, 'young' idiot and got into that very common and frustrating cycle of easing off running, then returning to test it, feeling it get inflamed again and repeat. I didn't give it the time to heal properly, and didn't return to running gradually enough with very cautious and progressive loading.

The first event of 2010, post the London Marathon, was a return to the Bala middle-distance race in mid-June. I knew my run wasn't in the shape of a year ago, but I went in hopeful of repeating the previous success. I swam and rode faster than in 2009, but the run was slower due to the lack of training, and I ended up 5th in my age group. I had one more race before heading down to the Alps, which was the Cowman middle-distance race at Milton Keynes. Another lacklustre performance, especially on the run, didn't provide the confidence boost I was hoping for.

During this period, my career took an about turn. One sunny day in May, I was in the garden painting our shed when I took a call on my mobile. It was an old colleague of mine from NatWest Markets/RBS, Brian Perry, who asked what I was up to. I explained I was painting the shed, and he replied, 'No, what are you really up to nowadays?'

Painting the shed, I replied. Brian laughed and went on to explain that he had moved from RBS and was now at the US investment bank, Morgan Stanley, and he thought I should come in to talk to them about a potential role. I wasn't mad keen as I had thought I had left the world of finance behind, but I said I'd think about it and let him know. I sat down with Luce when she came home from work and we discussed it over dinner, the conclusion of which was why not go and have a chat. I was acutely aware that I hadn't managed to find a role in conservation and that I wasn't contributing financially.

Coincidentally, around this time, I was also contacted by a headhunter who I had worked with previously, about a potential role at Bank of America. In for a penny in for a pound, I thought and decided I may as well have a chat with them as well. Anyway, to cut a long and dull story short, after many interviews, both institutions offered me a job. I hadn't been expecting this and had another chat over dinner with Luce asking her advice for what to do. Morgan Stanley, MS, was a more prestigious institution, and I preferred the people I had met there, but it would mean commuting to Canary Wharf[7].

The Bank of America job was a better commute, based near St Paul's, but I wasn't that impressed with the guy I'd be working for. Luce advised I take the MS role and, on balance, I agreed it was the best choice. To be honest, I can't think of an occasion when her advice wasn't the right course of action. So, I was heading back into investment backing approximately 18 months after leaving it with my grand flouncing out of the meeting at RBS.

This didn't sit well with me, I felt like I had failed with the plan to shift careers into doing something more meaningful, but I needed a job and wasn't sure what else to do. But first, I had Alpe d'Huez to race, so I agreed with MS that I'd start on August 1st once I returned from my July trip to the Alps.

I was nervous and excited about Alpe d'Huez. It would be the longest race I had ever done, and in very unfamiliar terrain, having not spent any time riding in the mountains. In 2009, I participated in l'Etape du Tour, which finished at the top of Ventoux, which was a fantastic but humbling experience. Climbing Ventoux in the heat that day had almost broken me, and given this was my only experience of riding up a big hill, I wasn't sure how I was going to cope with the Alpe d'Huez race, which had three significant climbs. Training in Hertfordshire really didn't provide decent preparation, either for climbing or descending, but I did what I

---

[7] This is a right royal pain in the arse from St Albans so I was aware it would make what would be already very long days, even longer

could with, for example, repeated efforts up Bison Hill.

We had decided to drive down to the Alps and were going to be spending time with friends Kris, Claire and James, the latter of whom was also doing the race. We stayed in Alpe d'Huez and spent some glorious days riding before the race. It was our first time riding in the Alps, and we fell in love with it. The race was a fantastic experience, albeit brutal, commencing with a very chilly 2.2km swim in the Lac du Verney.

The bike course was even more spectacular than I imagined, kicked off with a fast 20k to the bottom of the first climb, Alpe du Grand Serre, which had an average gradient of 6.5% over 15km. I was feeling good and loving the steady, largely wooded climb, taking particular pleasure from overtaking one of the athletes that I'd seen blatantly draft in Australia the previous year. A rolling section then took us to the next climb, the Col d'Ornon, which had no tree cover unfortunately, given the temperature had risen significantly by now.

The subsequent descent was eye-opening and terrifying. I watched in awe as riders came screaming past me on the technical, twisty descent into Bourg d'Oisans. I was well aware of my bike handling limitations, even on the road bike I had chosen to ride, but this experience was taking it to a new level.

A feeling of deep relief at still being alive washed over me as I made it onto the valley floor and headed to the bottom of Alpe d'Huez. I can remember my hands hurting from the amount of braking down the descent; such a wuss. Alpe d'Huez is tough on its own, averaging 8% over almost 14km, but having a fair bit of climbing in the legs already made it feel like purgatory. The bottom section around the first few hairpins is particularly steep and I did start to have doubts about whether I'd make it. The heat was now feeling extreme, and I'd run out of fluid, but I got my head down and just started counting down the hairpins.

Thankfully, there was an aid station near what is known as 'Dutch corner', so I grabbed a bottle and some food and pressed on. Reaching the summit was a huge relief until I started to think about the 20km run to come. My transition was terrible. I haven't ever felt so immobile getting off the bike in T2, but I told myself it would get better and headed out on the 3 laps, hilly run. I hadn't really thought about running at altitude and quickly found each climb to feel increasingly challenging, but at this point, it was all about simply finishing, which I finally did in just over 7 hours. I felt elated to have completed such an epic race, and it was definitely the hardest race experience to date.

The long drive home to the UK gave me plenty of time to think about the forthcoming return to the world of finance, which I was feeling very apprehensive about. Morgan Stanley had a formidable reputation and together with Goldman Sachs, was probably the pre-eminent investment bank. I really wasn't sure I would be able to cut it or would find it a miserable existence, so I arrived home with some trepidation about what was to come.

There is no doubt that triathlon took a back seat from August 2010 for a while. Trying to establish myself at MS whilst suffering once again from major imposter syndrome required some commitment and energy, with very long days inevitably resulting in a much lower training volume. I was determined to keep up the training and racing but decided to go back to focusing on sprint and

Olympic distances only, at least until I felt more established at work. I also decided to work with a coach for the first time as I thought I needed to maximise every minute of the few training hours I would have available.

Finding a coach wasn't a particularly rigorous process. Some surfing on the web quickly alighted on Bill Black, who was also coaching a very talented guy in my age group. Bill was very experienced, coaching the men's triathlon team at the Sydney Olympics in 2000 and also coaching the ex-world champion Spencer Smith. We had an introductory call, and I immediately felt like we'd get on, which was the most important factor for me.

Very affable, slightly quirky with a great sense of humour, but with years of triathlon wisdom to impart, the relationship with Bill quickly blossomed. He did a great job at devising a programme which fitted within my very busy week yet still provided enough stimulus for development.

A typical week at this point averaged approximately 6-8 hours of training. The alarm went at either 5 am or 5:15 am, and a finely honed routine of breakfast, showering, and shaving allowed me to jump on a train at around 6:15 am to London. The commute, as previously alluded to, was a pain, requiring a change on to the Jubilee line tube, resulting in me arriving at my desk at around 7:30-7:45 am if everything had gone smoothly.

In the first few months, there wasn't any time for training before work, although as I became more comfortable, I started to sometime squeeze a quick 30-minute swim in or run part of the way to work.

Working in the dealing room (my role was very similar to my

previous one at RBS, running a global quantitative advisory team) meant that there wasn't the really late nights that other parts of the bank would work, but I often wouldn't leave before 6 pm, meaning not getting home until somewhere between 7:30 and 8 pm depending on how useless the public transport system had been that evening. This only really allowed a quick bite to eat and, sometimes, a relatively short bike session on the turbo before getting into bed around 10-10:30 pm, ready to repeat it all the following day.

I didn't endure many of these weeks before I realised I was going to have to be uber-efficient if I wanted to keep training at a level to retain any form of competitiveness. Using the commute to run to work, usually once a week, became a staple of the weekly programme, with longer (approx. 10 miles) or shorter (approx. 6 miles) depending on how early I got off the train.

I also sometimes tried to run home but found that I was generally too tired and/or hungry at the end of the day, and the sessions were less effective than in the morning. I have always been a morning person. I also tried a couple of times to ride to work and use the commute to get some bike volume done (it was approx. 26 miles one way), and it was usually ok in the morning as I would be so early, until getting into Central London anyway, but the evenings were carnage. Traffic around 5:30-7 pm coming out of London was horrendous, and after a couple of near misses and much frustration getting stuck in jams, I decided to bin the bike commute idea.

Finishing off the 2010 season, I completed another couple of Olympic distance races at Bedford and Bala. The Bala race was once again a happy hunting ground, winning my age group in just under 2:02 and getting a £200 cheque for the privilege. Although it was still early days, this result did give me some confidence that I may be able to still race competitively and work at Morgan Stanley. The season wrapped up with a 2-week break from training in October when we headed off to Africa to climb Mount Kilimanjaro, which was an incredible experience.

However, in hindsight, I found this climb tougher than the Alpe d'Huez triathlon, suffering badly from altitude sickness and only just making the summit. One of our friends, sadly, didn't summit and had to be evacuated on the last day when he collapsed, also from the effects of altitude.

The work week whilst in London was pretty full on, but this was compounded by the fact that my role would require a lot of international travel. My previous roles had also required a fair bit of travel but it increased significantly over the following few years. There were regular trips to European cities that were often day trips, which I would find frustrating as they would be enforced rest days as they would typically start with a trip to Heathrow at 5 am and often not getting home until 9-10 pm. Longer trips to North America and Asia, for 1 or 2 weeks, were also pretty common, and I became a master of planning and efficiency in order to squeeze training in every slot I possibly could.

This planning would commence as soon as I was told I needed to travel somewhere that would require overnight stays. I asked my assistant, who would book flights and hotels, to try to only book hotels off the preferred supplier list that had a pool and gym.

Some of these hotel pools were pretty terrible, but I got used to being flexible and adapting session structures and durations according to what was available. If I was going to be away for a weekend, which was less common, I would look into bike hire in the city I'd be staying in.

Luckily, I could afford to be efficient here and use companies who would drop the bike at my hotel, and then pick it up when I was leaving. This resulted in some great rides in Melbourne, Sydney, Auckland and New York, although bike training whilst travelling was typically confined to using gym bikes. Running was obviously easier to fit in, and I would normally aim to get a run in before breakfast, which required pre-planning a snack in the hotel room for when the alarm went off at 5 am (I'm not a fan of running on a totally empty stomach and have found that I at least need a coffee and something small if I'm going to make the session half decent).

Many evenings, at the end of long days of meetings, I have ducked into late-night shops to pick up a snack for the room for the following morning. Again, this has resulted in me running in many major cities around the world, from Barcelona, Frankfurt, Stockholm, Boston, Miami, LA, New York, Toronto, San Francisco, Chicago, Singapore, Sydney, Brisbane, Tokyo, Hong Kong to Baltimore, Abu Dhabi and Melbourne.

The jet lag often meant running around some of these cities at unusual times of day, and one of the favourite routes became a 4 am loop of Central Park in New York. It never ceased to surprise me how many others I'd see running or riding around the park or how many critters, such as raccoons, I'd bump into.

I became ridiculously efficient, much to the bemusement of many of the work colleagues that I'd travel with. There is no doubt that I was looked upon as a bit odd, not just from the training perspective but also as I would try to avoid some of the work social events, partly as I wanted to use the time to train or recover, but also because I am an introvert at heart. A day of client meetings and having to talk all day, often presenting complex topics and getting grilled accordingly, would mentally exhaust me, and I just didn't want to talk to anyone else by the end of the day.

Many of the trips to the US would be a city per day, flying to the next one in the evening, so a schedule might be Boston-New York-Baltimore-Chicago-San Francisco-LA and then home. If I knew the program before leaving the UK, then I would pre-schedule what training I could although sometimes the itinerary would change at the last minute, or even be unknown at the time I was leaving the UK. This would drive me absolutely mad as I hated not knowing what I was doing in which location on what day, and it would test my flexibility to the maximum!

Lesson: no matter how busy you are, it is possible to do what you love, you just need to prioritise, plan and be efficient.

Nerves

I've now completed many races, and I can safely say, I have felt at least some nerves prior to the start of every one. I agree with the widely quoted sentiment that the day you stop feeling nervous, you should probably seek another hobby, as they are a sign that what is about to come matters to you. Yes, some races have resulted in more nerves than others, and a return to the World Championships in London in 2013 was probably the race where I suffered the most from pre-race anxiety and pressure.

The 2011 season felt like I was treading water, not literally, although my swim speed could be viewed as this. Triathlon was still important to me, but I was still trying to establish myself at work, which was becoming quite all-consuming. I entered a few sprint and Olympic distance races, but the season didn't start well. At the local Merchant Taylors Olympic race I suffered my first DNF, getting a puncture just 400m coming out of T1.

This was the first time I had raced with a disc wheel, and stupidly, I did not have a spare tube with the right length valve to fit the disc. As Lucy will testify when I do something really stupid, I tend to get very angry with myself for such stupidity, and that day was no exception. As I cursed on the side of the road another competitor rode by, laughing and asking me, without too much sincerity, if I was ok and did I need any help. This didn't improve my mood, and I trudged back to transition.

The season didn't improve at the next race, the picturesque Dartford Bridge Olympic race, situated next to the M25. Having ensured I had the appropriate spare tubes, I was fully fired up to make amends and swam well, for me, until the end of the course. Coming into the swim exit, my extended hand hit the wooden pontoon right on the end of my fingers at speed (the very murky water didn't allow for too much visibility), and I thought, ouch, that hurt.

I knew something wasn't quite right as I dragged myself onto the pontoon and was distraught to look down and see one of my fingers at right angles, very badly dislocated at the first knuckle. I ran to a St John's Ambulance guy, with spectators saying 'oooo' as I went by, and pleaded with him to put my finger back in. He said he wasn't allowed to, which I didn't understand, so I tried tugging on it myself.

It wasn't budging, and I knew at this point I wouldn't be able to carry on as I was going to struggle to get my wetsuit off, never mind ride a bike and be able to use the brakes. Off we went to a local A&E to get it sorted, which required 2 nurses yanking it with some gusto whilst sucking on gas and air. I wasn't sure what was more painful, getting the finger back in or a second consecutive DNF.

The next race wasn't for another 2 months, returning to the old favourite, Milton Keynes, at the end of July, which was hosting the English National Championships this year. I finally managed to finish a race in just under 2:02 again, getting bronze in the process. The next couple of races also went ok, getting third in the age group at Hyde Park and winning at the Cambridge Olympic race in August.

A couple of sprints finished the season, including the local Tri-Force club championships, which I won, and the season was over.

Training volume had increased a little as I became more efficient at fitting it in, averaging approximately 10 hours per week in 2011 and 2012.

The following year delivered a milestone at work, a promotion to Managing Director in January. At an institution such as Morgan Stanley, being a Managing Director was a big deal and the process of getting such a promotion was long and rigorous, with numerous stages with less than 200 individuals globally promoted every year. I was chuffed as it did mark a key moment for me, the hard work from August 2010 onwards had made an impact, and I felt much less of an imposter. I had one of my bosses, Oliver Jerome, to thank as I was well aware of how hard he had lobbied for me, and such a sponsor was critical in order to be successful.

2012 was another unremarkable triathlon season, which kicked off again in the spring with another return to the London Marathon. The goal was sub 3, and I went through halfway on target, but the wheels fell off around 18-20 miles, and I ended up with 3:04 and another sore achilles. I decided to hang up my marathon boots, thinking that marathons weren't fundamentally very good for you, or at least, for an increasingly middle-aged man's achilles. Once healed up, I did manage 37:09 at a 10km race that May, and also ran a half marathon PB at the Great North Run in September, finishing in just over 1:20, but I seemed to struggle to stay injury-free when ramping up the volume for the marathon distance.

The tri season was nothing special, commencing with racing the Slateman race in North Wales in May. I didn't particularly enjoy the race; the water was absolutely freezing (I suffer badly in the cold, a trait that would only get worse as I got older), and the run was bonkers. Out of T2, you basically ran up what felt like the vertical side of a slate mine and then descended down some steep trails to the finish. I am no mountain goat and remember getting passed by many, typically hairy, fell runner types on the technical descent. I managed to sneak onto the age group podium but vowed I wouldn't be doing any more races that involved such off-road style running.

I raced the British and English National Olympic Distance Champs that summer at Shropshire and Milton Keynes, respectively. In both races, I finished in 2 hours and a few seconds, but this only got me 5th and 4th place, which felt like a step backwards. The stress of work and the reduced training volume had resulted in me slipping down the age group a little, but at least I was still racing. I did start to find more training time as we bought a flat in London that year, which we stayed in during the week in order to reduce the time spent commuting (which could be up to 3 hours per day from St Albans).

Getting to work now involved a 25-minute ride on a 'Boris bike,' which I really enjoyed as most of the journey was on a cycle lane. Many evening commutes involved hammering home on the unwieldy bike, trying to beat my best times for various segments, although particular satisfaction was always had when overtaking folks on normal bikes (even someone on a TT bike one day, which I think went down like a cup of cold sick as he came tearing by me a few minutes later).

Heading into the winter, I had mixed feelings about the year – I had set new run PBs in all distances and was managing to complete Olympic distance triathlons in 2 hours, but I still felt like I had been treading water to some extent. World Triathlon had announced that the World Championships were going to be in London the following year, and I thought this was an opportunity that I could not miss. I decided to put my drafting indignation from 2009 behind me and fully commit over the winter to try to qualify. It was going to be extremely competitive, and although I was going up to the 45-49 age group in 2013, I was well aware that I wouldn't be able to tread water as I had over 2011-2012.

As we always did, Luce and I sat down to plan the season of racing over the winter. The strategy was to try to qualify early again, even though the first qualifier always had the most stacked field. My view was that if I was going to go well at the World Championships, I'd have to race all the best guys in 45-49 anyway, so why not just see where I was early on? The first qualifier was the Deva race in Chester on the 2nd of June, so I raced a couple of sprints beforehand to blow the cobwebs away, practice transitions and remember what race intensity felt like. I'd had a good winter, injury-free and consistently managing to average just over 11 hours of weekly training, which was a small increase from 2012. Work was even more intense with the promotion, and I was also studying for my British Triathlon coaching qualifications, but the reduced time spent commuting made a big difference.

I remember feeling very nervous the night before Deva. We'd driven up the day before to recce the bike course and get a feel for the race environment. I'd looked at the start list, which was as rammed as I was expecting, and the familiar feeling coming out of a winter's training was present in that you just don't know how you're going to stack up against the competition. I knew I'd had a decent winter, including a PB of 35:57 at the Bupa 10km the

Monday before the race, but you didn't know if your main competitors had had better ones!

The swim at Deva is in the river Dee, heading upstream for the first 800-900m, which can feel like hard work. Swimming as far to the bank as I could to avoid the strongest section of the current, I got stuck in and tried to relax. I had stopped wearing a watch when racing, which I've found to be particularly beneficial for the swim leg as you never know the exact distance, impact of currents etc, so the absolute time is irrelevant. And on days like this, it was all about age group placing, with the top 4 gaining an automatic qualification slot for the World Champs. I came into T1, after a steep uphill run from the river, in 11th, which I was pleased with, given the size and quality of the field. It was another magic day on the bike, taking the lead by passing Alan Rowe after about 25km or so and setting the fastest bike split in the age group. Although Alan came back at me on the run, I managed to hold on and won the age group by approximately 30 seconds. It felt like Little Beaver in 2009, qualification done and dusted at the first outing, and I was chuffed to bits. It would now allow me to fully focus on getting in the best shape I could for Hyde Park in September.

There wasn't a lot of time until the next race, the European Champs in Alanya, Turkey, on the 14th of June. This was another great trip and another dream achieved, claiming silver in the 45-49 age group, a first international podium. A non-wetsuit swim didn't get the race off to a great start, but a flat bike leg up and down a dual carriageway helped compensate for the swim deficit. I came onto the run in the bronze position, with Lucy and our friend Sam (who also happened to be one of British Triathlon's sports therapists) screaming at me as I headed out of T2 onto a very hot run. The 3 lap course included a short but steep hill, and on the third lap, I finally came up behind the Italian chap in second.

Knowing I was relatively strong on hills, I decided to make my move and came by him on the incline, desperately trying to conceal the fact I was blowing out of my arse. I imagine this was an abject failure, but I didn't look back, crested the hill and tried to pick it up. I managed to hang on to silver by 15 seconds and was ecstatic. My nemesis from previous age group racing, Olaf, won by 3 minutes (he'd put 4 minutes into me on the swim), and the score moved to Olaf 2, Pete 0, but I didn't care at all. The goalposts, which had originated at just qualifying to race for Great Britain and then moved to, maybe, one day, getting on a podium at an international event, were going to have to shift again.

Races came thick and fast that summer, with a return to the Dambuster race only the following weekend, which was hosting the English National Champs that year. In hindsight, I don't think I'd fully recovered from Turkey, but I managed to grab bronze after getting taken on the run by a rival, Steve McKeown, whom I'd got to know a little. Steve was a fantastic athlete and a particularly strong runner, so when he came cruising by me on the run, saying, 'Stay with me Pete,' I had to stifle a chuckle, and I think I just about managed to utter 'yeah, right' in reply. Our rivalry was due to be renewed only 3 weeks later at the British National Champs in Liverpool.

Liverpool was probably the best Olympic distance performance I have managed to put together. Again, we'd travelled up the morning before the race and spent a sunny Saturday afternoon watching the locals prepare for their night out, festooned in hair curlers whilst sitting in the pub.

Although the season was going better than I could have ever expected, Dambuster had revived some doubts, and the usual nerves were present. In these situations, I have always had the great fortune of having Luce as a sounding board and source of motivation and wisdom. I knew Steve was on the start list (he hadn't raced at Deva) and I don't think I'd ever beaten him at this point. Chatting over dinner, Luce simply and calmly said, 'He's beatable,' but with such conviction that I actually allowed myself to believe it. Maybe.

The swim in Liverpool docks went ok, coming out 15th in the age group, and headed out on to the 2 laps of a dual carriageway bike course. I had come to learn that this sort of course should play to my strengths, and it was once again proved correct. I clocked 56:33 for the 40km (but I think it was slightly short), the fastest split in the age group, which saw me heading out of T2 in the lead.

The run course was also slightly short and comprised of 2 flat laps, with turnarounds so you could clock your competition. I knew there would be a rapid Steve McKeown running me down, and I was hoping that I had put enough time into him on the bike to hold him off, unlike at Dambuster.

We acknowledged each other at the turn with a nod and brief 'Steve', to which he responded 'Pete'. I don't think the effort level allowed for anything more verbose. I could see he was slowly gaining on me, but by the final turnaround, I was starting to believe I was going to hold on, which I managed to do, claiming the National AG title for the Olympic distance for the first time. I'd run 35:26, finishing in just under 2 hours and winning by approximately 50 seconds. Mum and Dad had come to watch but missed the finish unfortunately! It was a great day, a race performance that still makes me proud, and the momentum towards the world champs was building.

I had decided as soon as I had qualified at Deva in early June that there probably wouldn't be another home world champs for a very long time if ever, given how hard it seems to be to host events that require closed roads in the UK, so I had to throw everything at it. I started biking the Hyde Park course once a week before work from our flat in Clerkenwell, and although I couldn't recce the whole course exactly, I did get very familiar with the sections in the park.

I also decided to try something different during the summer, taking advantage of the newly opened Altitude Centre in London, which provided a facility where you could bike or run in a room with a lower oxygen concentration in order to simulate altitude training. I bought 8 sessions and did a bike or run session one evening each week leading up to the World Champs, with the last one at the beginning of the taper week before the race.

I didn't know much about altitude training, and in hindsight, I probably should have stopped the sessions a bit earlier, but I felt like I was doing everything I could to be as fit as possible. I also spent a lot of time practising cornering on my TT bike as I was aware the course was pretty technical, and bike handling was going to be key.

Nerves were jangling heading into race week, partly due to the pressure I was putting on myself. This was partly due to the success of the season so far, and expectations were high, even though when

I checked the very large start list, it was clear that a Top 10 finish would require one hell of a performance on the day.

Pressure was also coming from my desire to not let down a large number of family and friends who were planning to come to watch. It was going to be the largest crowd of supporters I would ever have at a race, some of whom were travelling a long way, and although I'm sure they wouldn't have felt it, I definitely felt the need to try and deliver a performance worthy of all their effort. I was humbled that so many people were coming to watch me swim, ride and run around Hyde Park.

Race morning finally dawned, and it was cold and foggy. The fog resulted in a delayed start, and we sat around trying to stay warm, waiting for updates. This delay certainly contributed to even more nerves, and it was a relief when they finally announced the race would start, albeit with a shortened swim to 750m due to the cold air temperatures.

The age group was split into two waves as it was so large, and I was off in the first wave. I didn't have a great swim, coming out in 11:34, but luckily wasn't aware as I didn't wear a watch and headed off on the bike. I didn't feel my usual self on the bike, but I rode as hard as I could, trying to ride the technical sections as well as possible, which wasn't very well as it happened. A GB teammate of mine, Richard Ashton, who was local to me and someone I'd raced many times over the years, said to me after the race that he saw me on the bike heading into one of the technical sections near Buckingham Palace.

Apparently, he thought to himself, 'Ah, there's Pete, he knows what he's doing on a bike, I'll follow his line' but then rapidly regretted this decision as he realised too late that I'd overcooked it, and therefore so did he, shouting 'fuuuucccck' as he just managed to avoid the hay bales stacked on the corner. Out of 163 starters in my age group, my bike split was on the 9th fastest, and I was slower than several guys who I'd outridden for the last couple of years.

The crowds on the 2 lap run course were incredible and I could hear the crowd that came to support me from a long way away. There is no doubt they lifted me on the run and I felt lighter coming by them on each lap, and also very emotional. The blue carpet of the finishing chute finally came into view, and I emptied myself, knowing that seconds were going to separate places, crossing with a 37:46 run split. I finished 14th in the end and promptly burst into tears with pent-up emotion when greeted by my family and friends as I exited the finish area. It was a fantastic event, a World Championships on home soil, in front of so many people I cared about, and I'd given it everything.

Once I'd had time to let the result sink in, I was disappointed not to get closer to the podium, but I think a factor in this was letting the event and result almost matter too much to me, the nerves didn't work in my favour and probably were a performance hindrance. I had plenty of time to cogitate on it as I flew to San Francisco for work the following day[8] and decided to try to manage the nerves better going forward. I also decided that my swim wasn't ever going to be strong enough for me to compete for international age group honours at the Olympic, or sprint, distance

---

[8] And was promptly very ill – I have memories of wandering with a raging fever around San Fran at 3am in the morning looking for a pharmacy for some medication

racing and that going forward, I was going to focus on the middle distance, or half Ironman, racing, where the swim was a smaller overall component.

Lesson: Some nerves are good, but they need to be channelled appropriately; when possible, you need to get 'the butterflies all flying in the same direction.'

Specialisation

Over the winter of 2013/14, the plan to specialise in middle distance racing firmed up, and I decided to kick the season off with a first foray into the world of Ironman, entering the 70.3 (or half ironman) race in Majorca in early May. I'd already dabbled at the distance, racing Vitruvian in 2008 and the Bala Middle race in 2009 and 2010, and thought that the relatively shorter swim component and longer bike, would play to my strengths. I didn't increase the training volume significantly, rising to an average of just under 12.5 hours per week in 2014, from approximately 11.5 hours per week in 2013.

Preparation over the winter was going well, entering a number of running races which indicated I was in decent shape (37:19 at the Serpentine 10k, 1hr for the local Fred Hughes 10 and 1:21 for Watford Half), but at the Bramley 10 in mid-February, I felt my achilles tighten up. In wonderful hindsight, I should have just stopped and walked home, but I eased up and jogged the last 30 minutes. Little did I know that achilles issues were going to plague my entire season.

I didn't run for the week following the Bramley race and decided to test it on the Saturday, as it felt like it had improved over the week when walking around. However, running with Luce on that Saturday morning was a dumb idea, and it was clear straight away that it wasn't ok. I stopped running again for 10 days and tested it again in early March, but knew it still wasn't healed, so I finally booked to see a physio on March 5th, who said it was either tendonosis of the tendon sheath, or a small tear of the tendon itself.

Only a scan would determine the issue, so I booked in for one on March 7th, and it was subsequently confirmed that it was a small tear and that I would be off running for at least 6-8 weeks. I was gutted. Gutted that I couldn't run, but also just annoyed at myself for not just getting it seen to immediately after Bramley and faffing around for 3 weeks thinking it would sort itself out.

Any period away from running has been a struggle for me, ridiculously, it has always made me feel that I'm not a 'proper' triathlete, although as I've got older, I've learnt to deal with it better. I focused on the swim and bike over this period, and religiously followed the rehab program prescribed by the tendon specialist, which involved a lot of isometric exercises under very heavy load.

I was given the all clear to try a short, easy run on April 17th, and after warming up on the bike, the relief at feeling no issues over the 13-minute run was immense. It was less than a month to Majorca 70.3, but at least I could now slowly build back. Looking back at my training diary, I was careful on the return to running for the first week or so, but started to try to increase the intensity soon after that. Again, not the smartest decision that season.

We headed off to Majorca on May 4th, looking forward to a week in the sun. We'd been to Majorca before, on a riding holiday back in 2011 (when it had snowed), but we had fallen in love with the island. We hadn't spent any time in the north of the island before, so we were looking forward to exploring around Alcudia, where the race was based. I knew I wasn't run fit, but I was swimming and riding well, hitting 343 watts for the hour the week before we travelled. This wasn't far off my best ever 60-minute watts, and it was a first sign that I seemed to be a volume responder when it came to bike training.

The week prior to the race was lovely, staying at a hotel adjacent to transition, which would become a theme over the years of racing abroad. Luce's race holiday planning is second to none in terms of ease of logistics. The swim course was marked out early, and I swam 28 minutes for a familiarisation swim on the Thursday, which was a significant confidence boost. We also rode the bike course, which was beautiful, kicking off with a rapid 20km to the bottom of the climb, followed by a twisty descent before a flattish last 40km. Even without the optimal run preparation, I was excited for the race, soaking up the Ironman atmosphere, which was buzzing and not anything I'd experienced before.

Race day dawned, and the weather was stunning. Little wind resulted in a pancake flat and warm Alcudia bay, and a 27:21 swim split for me, which was a PB. Headed off on the bike like a loon and quickly decided that I liked Ironman events, especially the quality of the organisation and the closed roads. I was going well on the bike, and even descended reasonably well (although I was overtaken by a fair number of guys), before it all went a bit wrong. Coming off the descent, heading down a country lane at around 30 mph, my front tyre blew and I almost shat myself. I managed to slow without coming off and stood angrily at the side of the road, trying to compose myself.

Once I'd stopped shaking, I focused on getting a new tube in. It seemed to take ages, and I tried not to let my head go down as riders went tearing by me. I finally got the new tube in and then struggled to get the CO_2 canister to inflate it to engage. A local farmer was leaning over his gate on the opposite side of the road, watching my increasingly agitated faffing, and decided to try to help, shouting 'vamos' loudly at me. This didn't really help, and I muttered 'I am bloody vamoosing' to myself as I finally got my second cartridge to engage and inflate the front tyre. I managed to screw this up though and didn't get the tyre to anywhere near the right pressure but thought 'sod it' and rode off, smiling sweetly at the farmer and thanking him for his help. I hadn't ridden a bike before with such little pressure in the front tyre and quickly discovered that going round corners was very hairy. I was frustrated and irritated, but I tried to concentrate and finally made it back to T2.

Afterwards, Luce told me that I exited T2 at speed and was clearly running angry. I felt surprisingly good on the run and managed to claw back a fair few places that I'd lost due to the puncture, finishing in just under 1:29 on a hot day with the 4th fastest run in the age group. This gave me 4:44 overall and 13th in the AG, which I was pleased with given the circumstances – I could see from my bike computer that the puncture took approximately 10-11 minutes to sort out[9], but I thought the chance of getting a slot for the 70.3 world championships had gone.

Qualifying for the Ironman, either full distance or 70.3, world championships is very different from qualifying for the championships I'd done to date, under the auspices of the sports governing body, now known as World Triathlon. It is unfortunate that triathlon is as fragmented as it is, with Ironman running its own championships alongside those of the governing body, and

---

[9] I know, this is an appallingly slow puncture repair

even further complicated today with the addition of SuperTri and the Professional Triathlete Organisation's (PTO) T100 championships. For the sake of the long-term future of the sport, I think all the various organisations need to get together and try to formulate some sort of plan to consolidate and simplify the championship structure. If they want to attract non-triathletes into the sport, there needs to be more clarity and simplicity. Anyway, back to Majorca.

For Ironman championships, all of their races around the world have a number of world championship slots, with the exact number per age group pro-rated depending on the size of the specific age group relative to the entire field. So, for example, for the larger age groups, typically 40-44 and 45-49, there may be 5-8 slots, whereas for the 70-74 age group, there may only be 1.

To take a slot, you have to be physically present at the awards ceremony, which is normally later that day for a 70.3 race and the following day for a full Ironman. Even though I'd finished 13th, and there weren't 13 slots in my age group, we still went to the awards ceremony, held on the beach at Alcudia, later that afternoon as it may be possible to get a roll-down slot if some folks ahead of me had either already qualified, or simply didn't want to go.

The 70.3 world championships that year were going to be held in Mont Tremblant in Canada, which we were keen to go to as we wanted to combine the trip with visiting our friends, Dean and Sophie, just outside Montreal. The roll-down process kicked off, and there were guys not taking their slots. By the time the last slot in any age group came up, there was still a chance that the guy in

12th would take it, but he didn't, and I managed to snaffle the last slot. We were chuffed to bits and excited at the thought of returning to Canada later in the summer.

Next up was the English National Middle Distance Champs, to be held at Grafman in Cambridgeshire that year, which was nice and local. I raced Grafman a few times over the years and enjoyed it, a reservoir swim, a fast bike course and an undulating 2-lap run on mixed terrain. The race went well, and I won my age group and was 7th overall in 4:14.

As with Majorca, the day after the race, I was travelling for work, flying to the US on Monday morning. It was only 2 weeks to the next race, the standard distance European Champs in Kitzbuhel, Austria, which I had pre-qualified for by virtue of the silver medal in Turkey the previous year. Even though I had decided to focus on middle-distance racing, we decided to head over to Austria as it was somewhere we hadn't been and it looked stunning. So I arrived back from a busy week in the US on Friday and headed off to Austria the following day.

In hindsight, this schedule wasn't the smartest. Only two weeks in between races, interspersed with a busy and stressful work trip to the US, which will have compromised recovery, was probably a little ambitious and indeed proved to be the case, I think. I have heard many times over the years how important it is to make smart decisions, in all aspects of training and racing, and how these decisions can have significant impacts down the line. In terms of planning a season of racing, Lucy and I now have a rule that ensures at least 3 weeks between races, wherever possible, which has become more important to stick to as I've got older.

Kitzbuhel did not disappoint. It was a stunning part of the world, and we had a fantastic week leading up to the race, staying in a house right on the lake in which I'd be swimming. We went for a run on the Tuesday before the race, which was on a very hilly route (not much flat around Kitzbuhel), and I remember feeling a slight twinge in the achilles that I hadn't torn only a few weeks ago. It didn't seem to be significant, and I didn't feel any discomfort or stiffness leading up to the race, so I decided to get on with it. The race went ok, coming 9th, on a very technical course, and pre-qualifying for the following year. Olaf was there, coming 7th and made the score Olaf 3, Pete 0.

Arriving back from Austria, I was off on another work trip, this time to Lugano and Milan, before racing again only the following weekend at the local Cowman middle distance race. If two weeks between races was too short, then a week was definitely verging on the downright dumb, but that is with the wisdom of hindsight. I won my age group at Cowman, coming 7th overall again, but felt that my achilles tightened up on the run, which was partly on fairly rough trails. A sensible Pete would have stopped on the run and just walked to the finish, but I was in the lead and ego/stupidity took over, much to the detriment of the rest of the season.

Just over 2 weeks later, after 'testing' the achilles on a treadmill in a hotel gym in Frankfurt and finding that it hadn't just miraculously healed, I was back seeing the same tendon specialist in London and having a scan. Bizarrely, exactly the same diagnosis was received, a small tear in the achilles, almost identical in size to the one in the other tendon, and the same rehab program was prescribed. No running for 6-8 weeks, until pain free, and a program of strengthening using the same isometric exercises under very heavy loads. It was now July 17th, and I was gutted, again, as it meant that I wouldn't be competing at the 70.3 world championships in Canada, or the British National Champs in Aberfeldy, the following month, as I wouldn't even be able to run by then. Poor decision making in June had almost certainly contributed to this outcome including squeezing racing on 3 weekends out of 4 into a crazy work travel schedule and ignoring niggles in training.

I tried to refocus again, investing my energy into swimming and biking, and religiously following the rehab program. My first run back was 20 minutes at the end of August, and I was once again relieved to be pain-free so I embarked on a cautious rebuild. Luce and I started to look at the race calendar and see if there were going to be any opportunities to race again that year and salvage something from a frustrating season.

At the end of September, I raced the New Forest Middle, pain-free, and won my age group, so we decided to press ahead with a last race of the season at the European Middle Distance Champs, back in Majorca on 18th October. I submitted my name for a place, which unlike the Olympic distance qualification process, are allocated based on how close you are to the winner of your age group at any half ironman race that meets British Triathlon's criteria (e.g. the distances have to be accurate, there needs to be a minimum number of competitors etc).

It was the right decision. We had a long weekend in Peguera, in the south of the island, and it was lovely. The weather was fantastic, very hot, which meant a non-wetsuit swim, although after the success in Turkey, this no longer bothered me as much as it used to. A stunning, undulating bike course was great fun, and the run was simply holding on, given that the temperatures were now in the mid-30s. I was happy to be racing, happy to be injury-free and had a blast. Luce saw me in the post-finish recovery area and called me over to sadly report that 'I was Charles'[10]. I wasn't too disappointed as I was just happy to have raced again before the season ended and not had any achilles issues.

After a post-race burger and pina colada, which has also become a thing over the years, we headed back to the hotel. Lying on the bed, we could hear the awards ceremony about to start nearby as Luce was having another look at the results online. She suddenly leapt up and said, 'Get up, you've come 3rd, we need to get down to the awards. '

The guy who had been in 3rd place was in the age group below and had been erroneously put in my age group, but this had been corrected in the final results. We dashed off out of the room, hoping to be in time for the 45-49 awards, and arrived just in time to receive the bronze medal. I know, it was 'only' bronze, but it felt like a perfect end to what had been a challenging season. We flew back to the UK the following day, feeling satisfied, before I headed off for 2 weeks to Australia, New Zealand, Tokyo, Beijing, Hong Kong and Singapore for an end-of-season 'break.'

Putting the achilles frustrations to one side, I had enjoyed focusing on middle distance racing in 2014 and decided to carry on with this specialisation in 2015. I can also see from my training diaries that I had finally started to learn, at least a little, in that in January I had

---

[10] This had become a saying as I raced a guy many times who often seemed to come 4th in our age group, and was called Charles, so coming 4th was 'doing a Charles'

a niggle in the area where the calf joins the soleus, the gastroc soleus musculotendinous junction, and backed off the running, including aborting a 10 mile race where I could feel it in the warm up. This better decision-making allowed me to train consistently through the winter, and although I wasn't feeling 100% prepared, I was excited to kick the season off early at the Ironman Oceanside 70.3 race near San Diego in March. Lucy's brother was living out there, and we decided to combine the trip, flying over there for just over a week with her sister, Caroline[11].

The taper week went well, nothing remarkable, and I certainly felt that I wasn't at my peak, but little did I know that I was about to enter a purple patch that I wouldn't match for many, many years. The swim was uneventful, and it took me a while to warm up and get the legs going on the bike, but after about 30 minutes, I just seemed to take off. The course goes through the US Marine Base, Camp Pendleton, and it was great fun.

A few climbs but a rapid course, and I found myself, for the first time, overtaking female pros in the last 40 minutes of the ride. A 1:27 run backed up the fastest bike split, which won my age group and gave me a slot for the Ironman 70.3 World Champs that year, which were due to be held at Zell am See in Austria at the end of August. I was stunned and stoked to win at an Ironman event, and one as large and prestigious as Oceanside.

Next up was the European Middle Distance Champs, due to be held at Rimini in Italy at the end of May, and my podium at the end of 2014 had pre-qualified me for the race. Training went well through April and May, averaging around 13 hours per week, and

---

[11] Also know as The Caxster

it felt like I had built and progressed well from Oceanside. I was to be proved right. In the week before the race, we first met someone who would become a good friend, Alex Jones, who Lucy took pity on as he ate on his own at a restaurant one evening. Alex was competing for Great Britain for the first time and was travelling on his own, so we ended up spending some time getting to know him.

The weather on race day morning was awful. A squally wind made the sea angry, with large waves and rollers obscuring the sighting buoys from the beach, some of which were still getting moved after the race had started. Surviving the swim, I exited T1 in 7th place and out onto a bike course which went up a hill, turned round and came back down. I was relieved to find the rain had stopped as I headed out, but this didn't last long, and by the time I was descending, the heavens had opened, and the roads were flooded and very sketchy with debris getting washed off the hillsides. It wasn't the fastest ride, but I was relieved to still be upright and in contention, heading out of T2 in the bronze medal spot.

The rain dried up and was quickly replaced by very hot sunshine, which would turn out to be very beneficial. A flat 2 lap run along the seafront lay ahead, which provided the opportunity for plenty of splits to the leaders from Luce, although she did have to carefully position herself to be out of earshot of the family and supporters of the Irish guy that was leading the age group. I think I moved into the silver medal position sometime towards the end of lap 1, but wasn't making huge inroads to the gap to the leader. However, shortly coming out onto lap 2, Luce informed me that it looked like the leader was starting to cramp, which gave me a second wind, and I pushed on.

Coming back from the turnaround, the update was even more encouraging, 'he's walking,'[12] I heard from the side of the road. With about 2km to go, I took the lead, trying to look comfortable as I 'eased' by, when in reality I was absolutely hanging and breathing out of every orifice. I had to just hold on, and as I reached the final turn into the finishing chute, I allowed myself a quick glance over my shoulder to see if I needed to worry about a sprint finish. This would have been very unwelcome as the diesel-like nature of my physiology does not lend itself to any form of sprinting, so I was hugely relieved to see I was clear and could relax and enjoy the finishing moments. I ended up running 1:26:02 that day, winning the 45-49 middle distance European gold medal by 45 seconds.

Frustratingly, the results on the tracker were showing that an Italian guy had won, but it was clear he had only completed 1 lap of the run course. Luce had seen that no one in my age group had finished before me, so we were 99% confident that the title had been on, but it was only when the results were corrected whilst we sat having dinner that evening that we allowed ourselves to celebrate. The awards ceremony was a bit bizarre, held in a strange dingey club, but it didn't matter – it was a first age group international title and I couldn't have been happier. Those goalposts were going to have to shift again. We celebrated with Alex and a few others from the age group team, including Rich Munday, who had also won in the 35-39 category, and Neil Lewis.

Interestingly, it was this result that seemed to generate more

---

[12] Not that I ever wish ill-will to any of my competitors but in a tight race to hear that there was a chance to take the lead was always a boost

interest in my triathlon hobby at work. Returning to work on Tuesday and the news that I'd won a European Championship seemed to travel around the dealing room. I recall the Head of Sales coming to my desk and asking to look at the results, which he was surprised at, exclaiming 'but you weren't the fastest swimmer, biker or runner?!'. No, I replied, but the sport is triathlon, and the goal is simply to be the fastest across the combination, which is a delicate balancing act of energy conservation. He looked at me, a little blankly, patted me on the shoulder, said well done and wandered off.

The season had started well, and the purple patch continued into June, when the next race would be the inaugural Ironman 70.3 at Staffordshire. We spent the weekend with friends, Matt [13] and Katie, with whom we would share many triathlon and cycling experiences over the years. The week before the race, I was away with work in the US and had picked up a bit of a cold, and still wasn't feeling 100% the day before, but had no symptoms below the neck, so I decided to crack on. I was glad I did as the winning run continued, with another decent bike split allowing me to hold off a very fast running Rich Ashton (who had regretted following my bike line at the 2013 world champs). We headed to the awards as Matt had also had a good race, coming 13th in his age group and was in the mix for a roll-down slot for the world champs in Austria. He secured the slot, which wrapped up a satisfying and fun weekend, although I haven't been back to race Staffs since, as I found the logistics around the split transitions a right old faff.

---

[13] Luce got to know Matt from her work and he had also started triathlon. Katie, his newly wed wife in 2015, was also a cyclist and runner

Two weeks later, we were back at Grafman for the English middle distance champs, and confidence was high. Another strong bike split helped deliver a 4th consecutive age group win and wrapped up this 3-month purple patch, a run of results that wouldn't be repeated for many years. Looking back, I'm particularly proud of this period and these performances; the setbacks and frustrations of 2014 had been consigned to history, but I had learnt from them and had started to make smarter decisions. The decision to try and focus on becoming a middle-distance specialist also seemed to be the right one, and as I took a mid-season break at the end of June 2015, I eagerly looked ahead to standing on the start line at my first 70.3 World Champs in Austria at the end of August.

Lessons: make smart decisions, and early, accurate, expert diagnosis is essential

Adversity

Apart from some achilles injuries, I had had the good fortune of not suffering significant adversity so far during my triathlon journey, but a dramatic change of fortunes was looming around the corner. I am well aware how life is generally full of various ups and downs, and how you cope with the adversity of the downs is a key component of your character. This was going to be severely tested over the period 2017-2021, but first, another major work change was imminent.

During 2015, I was involved in many discussions at work about the potential to spin my team out of Morgan Stanley and set up a new business, which MS would partly own. The conversations were long and complicated, and became quite advanced by the summer of 2015, with the outcome looking increasingly positive during a number of calls I took on the subject whilst on a cycling holiday to Morzine in mid-July.

Prior to the holiday, I raced at the European Standard Distance Champs in Geneva, had a lovely time, came 9th and gave Olaf the opportunity to make the score 4-0, marking the end of my standard distance racing career. Whilst flying to and from the head office in New York to try to finalise the deal, I tried to focus on final preparations for the 70.3 World Championships in Austria.

I went into the race with no real idea of where I may come in my age group. I obviously knew that the standard of the field would be high, but it was new ground for me, and I was excited. The race was based in the town of Zell am See, which was absolutely stunning, especially as we were blessed with perfect weather.

Much to the pleasure of Luce, Javier Gomez, the Spanish professional, was staying at the same hotel as us. Javi must have started to become a little alarmed as we'd also bumped into him in the race hotel in Geneva in July, so unsurprisingly, he kept his distance from the two weirdo stalkers, which was a shame as he came across as a really lovely bloke.

The day kicked off well with a 29:29 swim in a crystal clear lake, before heading off down a very rapid start to the bike course for approximately 20km. The road then turned upwards, with a pretty significant climb for about 10-12km before a rapid descent and flat final section. I loved the bike course, rode it well in 2:25 and arrived back at T2 with no idea of where I was but full of endorphins.

The temperature had risen significantly by now, and the 2 lap run around the edge of the lake became a proper slog in the heat, but I held on to finish with a 1:34 run and 4:38 overall, which gave me 8th overall and the first Brit home in 45-49. I was chuffed to bits with the performance and the result, especially as it quickly became apparent that the depth of the field was much stronger at Ironman world championship events when compared to other events. Ironman championships are different from racing for your country under your National Federation but I thoroughly enjoyed the experience; the organisation and atmosphere were fantastic and would attract me back to race at this event many times in the future.

Although Zell am See marked the end of the triathlon season, which was probably a good thing as life at work was about to become a whole lot more stressful, we did have one more event to look forward to. Luce and I had joined up with a Morgan Stanley team to ride from London to Paris for the Blood Cancer charity in mid-September. It was a fantastic experience, even with the hideous weather on day 3 when it absolutely poured down for hours and I spent some time doing press-ups and getting man-hugs from one of the team members, Keith, to try to get warm at the rest stop. The final day riding into Paris was something I will never forget. We paused on the outskirts to wait for our police escort, who then proceeded to lead us into the city with a rolling road closure, shutting off junctions and roundabouts as we approached them. I cannot imagine ever doing anything like this in the UK, as the drivers just wouldn't tolerate it. Finishing off by riding up the Champs-Élysées, around the Arc de Triomphe and ending near the Eiffel Tower is a memory I will treasure for the rest of my life. It was magical and made even more so by sharing it with Luce.

I arrived back in the office from Paris to find that the powers that be at Morgan Stanley had decided that my team was no longer going to be spun out of the organisation. I was left with a decision to make; either I just accepted the decision and got my head down to carry on as before, or I took the much bigger risk, backed myself and resigned from the firm to set up on my own.

Two of my colleagues were keen to join me on the adventure, Ollie Jerome, who had been instrumental in my promotion to Managing Director in early 2012, and Aman Thind, who worked in technology and had been key in the success of delivering the products researched and designed by my team at MS. We spent time thrashing out the feasibility of setting up our own company, a financial software firm (or 'fintech' in the common parlance at the time) that would help investors save money by accurately measuring their transaction costs when investing in the markets.

Concurrent to these conversations, MS was going through a major reorganisation, and it became apparent that there may be an opportunity for Ollie and I at least to take voluntary redundancy.

Final decisions were made over a steak at Boisedale in Canary Wharf, where the three of us decided to go ahead as equal partners in a new company which we'd call BestX[14]. We agreed to self-fund the venture, with Ollie and I taking the voluntary redundancy on offer whilst Aman, who was based in New York, would resign in a couple of months time and join the new company when his non-compete period allowed. It was beyond me that MS were happy to offer me voluntary redundancy when only 3 months prior they had decided they weren't going to spin my team out as they didn't want me to leave, but it felt like the risk was worth taking.

A number of clients had said to me that they wanted me to set up a new company offering the product we were planning, but independent from a large bank, which gave me some assurance that there was demand. So, on December 8th, Ollie and I emptied our desks and left MS with a mixed set of emotions, some sadness as I had generally enjoyed working there, but also excitement and trepidation at what lay ahead.

BestX was founded on 26th January 2016, and after we'd filed at Companies House, we celebrated with lunch at J Sheekey, a city institution. If I thought work had been stressful before, I was about to experience a whole new level, with BestX rapidly becoming all-consuming. Although I'd worked long hours in previous roles and organisations, I had become better at compartmentalising, i.e.

---

[14] A financial term referring to 'best execution', meaning that when an investor trades in the market their goal is to attain the best possible execution of the trade e.g. minimising cost etc

leaving work at work when I did manage to leave the office and focus on home and training as required. But setting up your own company, and desperately wanting it to succeed, meant that compartmentalisation was kicked way into touch, and I found myself living and breathing BestX, at least for the first couple of years as we became established.

Aside from founding a new company, 2016 kicked off in a pretty terrible fashion with the death of David Bowie on 10th January. If anyone ends up reading this who doesn't really know me, they will probably find the rest of this paragraph pretty weird, but I was totally devastated and took some time to actually believe the news. I had been a huge fan since a very early age, probably around the age of 9 when I found the Changes One compilation album in my parent's record collection. I was intrigued and stuck it on the turntable, lay on the floor with some headphones on, and was blown away by the opening chords to Changes.

Bowie became a significant part of my childhood from then on, quickly exploring his back catalogue and having the good fortune of seeing him several times in concert, including the evening before my Maths A Level exam in 1987. On the 10th January, once it had been confirmed that he really had died, I decided to travel down to his birthplace in Brixton to pay my respects.

There were already crowds of people gathered outside, including several media crews, one of whom, from France, came over to me to interview me. I think they regretted their decision as soon as they asked their initial question, 'why have you come here today and what did David Bowie mean to you', and some sad middle-aged man burst into tears, trying to provide an inarticulate answer in between sobs, sniffles and snot. Funnily enough, they didn't ask me anything else, thanked me and quickly moved on to others in the crowd. I'm assuming this clip didn't ever air in France, although if it did, I'm not sure it would have done much to raise the French opinion of their neighbours across the Channel.

Since those dark days of January 2016, I've read many commentators lamenting the fact that the world has just gone pear-shaped since David Bowie died, and I couldn't agree more. Only a few months later we had the complete lunacy of the Brexit referendum result, followed by Trump the 1st, a global pandemic causing years of mayhem, the chaos of the Conservative government in the UK including Boris and Liz the Lettuce, the death of Queen Elizabeth, the Russian invasion of Ukraine, war in the Middle East, before the more recent return of Trump the 2nd. Not a great sequence of events.

The 2016 season was due to kick off with a return to Majorca in early May for the Ironman 70.3, where I felt I had unfinished business from the puncture in 2014. We had another lovely week riding the week before, but the weather on race morning was awful, with heavy rain and high winds. I had a decent swim and headed off on the now-familiar bike course in the pouring rain.

All was going ok whilst working hard on the flat and up the climb, but on the descent I started to get cold and couldn't stop shivering, to the extent that I was struggling to control the bike. By the time I was back on the flat, I tried to put some effort in to warm up but by then I was so cold it didn't make any difference, and the shivering and reduced power output persisted all the way to T2. I was annoyed and gutted, this race just seemed to be my bogey race, and was hugely relieved to get off the bike in transition, albeit in 13th place in the age group, and head out on the run. By this time, the rain had eased, and I ran angry, feeling good and moving through the field, to eventually claim 3rd with a 1:25 and a spot on the podium. The run had helped counter the disappointment of the conditions encountered on the bike, although I still felt, frustratingly, that I hadn't done myself justice at Majorca 70.3.

Two weeks later, we were back at Grafman for the British Middle Distance Champs, another race that had become familiar. I had a good day, winning my age group and happily taking another national title, although I was beaten on the bike by someone I hadn't heard of before. I came out of T2 a little way behind him, with accurate information from Luce, 'big guy, ginger beard', and got stuck in to try to chase him down, and a 1:26 run split was thankfully enough to claim the win. I have come to learn over the years that even if you study a start list prior to race day, there is always someone to surprise you, either a ringer who you've never come across, or someone you know who suddenly takes a performance leap forward.

In June, we headed back up to North Wales to race the Bala Middle Distance race. Training had been going well, whilst managing the stress of getting our first software product at BestX built, and I was looking forward to racing on a course I enjoyed with our friend, Matt. We were blessed with beautiful weather, a rarity we had come to discover in North Wales and had a lovely weekend. The race went well, finishing 2nd overall, which came as a bit of a surprise, to say the least.

At the finish, I'd gone to the timing company van to get my results, not really knowing where I'd finished, and the guy printed my bit of paper and said 'congratulations, you finished second'. I assumed second in the age group but then checked again and it was second overall, which resulted in my biggest triathlon pay cheque ever with a £500 prize. Post-race refuelling at Burger King at the motorway services on the way home was on me.

On a gentle short run a few days later along the Charles River in Boston (I had done my usual and planned a work trip post-race whilst recovering), I felt that my achilles wasn't quite right. I hadn't felt it during the race, but was immediately anxious given the experiences of 2014. Once back in the UK, I asked my GP to refer me to the same tendon specialist, Noel, I'd seen previously, who confirmed with a scan at the end of June that I had a small tear again in the right achilles and a small tendinopathy in the left. Gutted didn't come close, particularly since I had religiously stuck to the strength and conditioning protocol I had been given in 2014.

The Cowman race the following weekend was obviously not going to happen, although I did do the swim and bike, an experience I found very unsatisfying and wouldn't be keen to repeat. Noel was confident that I'd be running again after 6 weeks, given we'd diagnosed it early, which meant that the European Ironman 70.3 Champs in Wiesbaden in Germany, in mid-August may still be an option.

It was a Groundhog Day moment, but at least I knew now that if I followed the specialist's advice, I had some idea of what the recovery path would look like. As it turned out, it was a pretty much identical process, and I was able to do a short, gentle test the week before Wiesbaden, and both achilles seemed ok. We drove down to Wiesbaden, unsure whether I'd be finishing the race, but thought we may as well, given we wouldn't be able to get refunds on the race entry and hotel at this stage. The drive was memorable in that I remember getting a call from Barclays Wealth to confirm that they would be purchasing our BestX product, thereby becoming our first client. Given that we hadn't launched the product yet, which wasn't due to go live until later in September, it felt like this was a significant milestone.

The race itself wasn't a significant milestone. I had a shocking swim and rode the technical, lumpy bike course poorly. The only silver lining was that I had no achilles issues on the run and was able to finish, running a 1:30, which I was pleased with given the lack of running over the last 2 months, and finishing 7th in the age group, but a very long way off the podium and was even lapped on the run to complete the humiliation. At least I could now try and build a little towards the last race of the season, which was the European Middle Distance Champs, to be held at Walchsee in Austria on 4th Sep, where I had a title to defend.

We had thoroughly enjoyed our trips to Austria over the last 2 years, and were keen to explore another part of the country. Walchsee did not disappoint and was absolutely stunning, just as beautiful as Kitzbuhel and Zell am See. We were there with Matt and Katie, with Matt also racing, and also caught up again with Alex, whom we had first met in Rimini, and introduced us to another triathlon friend, Jack, for the first time. Coincidentally, this weekend also happened to be the weekend that our first product at BestX was formally going live into production, so there was quite a lot of time spent working and also on the phone on the days and evenings prior to the race.

Probably not the best preparation, and my mind was undoubtedly distracted, but I enjoyed the race; it would be hard not to in such a beautiful environment. I didn't come close to defending my title, coming 6[th,] but was happy to be injury-free and spending time with friends in a lovely part of the world. Sadly, one of the memories from the race was getting abused by another GB athlete, who came up to me at the finish area and started shouting at me for cutting him up on the bike.

Apparently, I didn't hold my line on a corner, which I don't recall, and generally, I'm pretty careful, but he was very irate. Luckily Matt was there to help defuse the situation as it became quite heated with me telling him to calm down and piss off. So, David Francis, if you ever read this, which of course is highly unlikely, I hope you've now managed to cool down and forgive me for whatever infraction I allegedly caused, although I don't seem to remember you coming off your bike or indeed having to amend your line at all.

Finishing the season as we went live at BestX was probably a blessing, as work took over for the remainder of 2016. There were many stressful days and evenings spent testing the product with a number of interested clients, whilst developing the next phase of the product roll-out and meeting with potential investors. They were all good problems to have, but the stress levels were high. We couldn't quite get our heads around the fact that we already had an interest in either investing in or acquiring BestX, a company that wasn't even 12 months old and wasn't generating any revenue yet. Indeed, the first interest came from a US private equity firm, which gave us a draft term sheet that summer, even before we had launched our first product. Needless to say, we politely declined as the terms were far from attractive.

2017 kicked off with BestX signing clients and generating revenue; the business was growing very fast, and life was full on. We were still not paying ourselves salaries, and only planned to do this when the company was firmly established and profitable, as we didn't want to have to take any external investment if possible. From a personal perspective, we decided to rent out our flat in Clerkenwell to generate some income during this phase, and so the long commutes returned, although at least only into the City and not Canary Wharf.

We decided to grab a few days of winter sun and headed off to Dubai to race the Ironman 70.3 there at the end of January. We're not fans of Dubai at all, finding it a very false and artificial place, but it was good to feel the warmth. The race went ok, grabbing another 3rd place behind a couple of nemesis, and noted, for the first time, that I probably didn't have the right gearing on my bike.

The out and back into the desert resulted in the homeward leg having a strong tailwind, and I found myself spinning out on several occasions, frustrated to see people flying by me with dinner plates for chain rings. Stupidly, it would take many years for me to correct this, although events over the next few weeks were going to push my bike gearing far from the top of my priority list.

One Tuesday in March, I happily did a usual training routine; a run to work which included some hill repeats up Primrose Hill, and then a short 40-minute swim at lunchtime. All was ok during the training, but I felt some chest pain later in the afternoon, but it didn't seem anything major, and I put it down to maybe pulling a muscle whilst swimming. I didn't experience any pain overnight or in the morning, so I headed off to the pool again. I was working from home on Wednesday, so I had the opportunity for a longer swim, performing the classic Swim Smooth 'Red Mist' session, which is comprised of 10 400m repeats, increasing the pace over the session. I felt good and had no issues, so I thought the previous day's pain was nothing to worry about. A tough sweet spot bike session that evening completed the day's training, pushing 292W and 301W for two 30-minute repeats on the Wattbike, and all went well. I recorded in my training diary, however, that the chest pain returned as I went to bed that evening, which was confusing, especially as I'd had such a good training day.

I was due to complete a tough early morning V02 run session on Thursday but had to miss it as I woke up with increased chest pain. In hindsight, I probably should have gone to the doctors at that point, but we had a busy day of client meetings scheduled, so headed into work as normal. By the time I got into the City, I was feeling decidedly uncomfortable, so I booked in to see a private GP, who seemed to think I was ok and sent me on my way. I managed to get through the morning, and Ollie and I headed off to Canary Wharf in the early afternoon to meet with HSBC to present BestX and potentially win what would be a huge client.

During the presentation, I had to stop my blethering, clutch my chest and exhale an expletive as the pain had suddenly become very intense. We abruptly ended the meeting, and I jumped into a black cab outside the HSBC office and asked to be taken to A&E at UCH, thinking that would be most convenient for Luce if she came into town. I thought I was having a heart attack, and I could tell from the cabbie's face that he thought the same. He did a fantastic job taking the back roads to try to avoid as much traffic as possible, but this did unfortunately involve going through a few traffic calming zones in residential areas, and every speed bump was excruciating, sending a stabbing pain in my upper left chest area.

Luce arrived at UCH A&E shortly after I did, and we sat in a crowded waiting room waiting to be seen. Cutting a long story a little shorter, after several hours of blood tests, waiting, a chest x-ray, more waiting, an ECG, more waiting, I was finally discharged at around 2 am with some ibuprofen with the final diagnosis being some sort of intercostal muscle issue. This didn't seem to quite fit, but we were told to go home, so we got a taxi home to St Albans, still somewhat bewildered about what was actually going on.

Funnily enough, things didn't improve over the next few days, and it clearly wasn't muscular. I worked from home on Friday but was getting increasingly breathless and feeling generally unwell. I remember doing a demo of our BestX product to Bank of America that afternoon and having to stop several times mid-sentence to catch my breath. I wasn't having the chest pain, but I was increasingly getting worried about the breathlessness.

By Sunday I was struggling to get up the stairs, so I booked an emergency GP appointment on Monday morning, who immediately sent me to A&E at Watford Hospital, phoning ahead to ensure I was seen quickly. The GP wasn't sure what the issue was, but thought it might be myocarditis, an inflammation of the lining of the heart.

Thankfully, Watford A&E seemed to take things a little more seriously, and I was seen immediately. When I described the events of the last few days, the consultant thought it sounded like it had started with a clot, although they were now concerned about my lungs. I was admitted and had a number of tests taken, including a sample of fluid from my lungs, which they sent off to try to figure out what was now causing a pretty serious chest infection.

The first night was spent on an acute medicine ward whilst they tried to find a bed on a ward, which was pretty grim, but it was going to get worse. Pressure to find beds for folks in A&E meant I had to be moved, and given the lack of beds, a consultant gave up his office and they squeezed a bed in there for me.

On one hand this was good as I didn't have to share the space with anyone else, but it also meant that I was not on the usual rounds, so was generally forgotten about a bit. I was on some major IV antibiotics and feeling very unwell, to such an extent that my memory of the next few days is patchy. I do remember falling out of bed to try to get to the toilet as I knew I was going to be sick, but didn't make it, threw up all over the floor and couldn't get up, so I just lay there for a while waiting for someone to come into the office. Grim. And this was 2017, way before the pandemic and the issues that the NHS has experienced since.

Luce was a legend throughout this period. It is so true that you tend to see people's true colours in times of need or crisis. Even though visiting times were quite restricted, Luce had sweet-talked the staff to let her sit in the office with me, with her laptop to notionally do some work, but just to keep me company, not that I was particularly entertaining to be around. Ollie visited, with cake, although I think for probably the first time in my life, I couldn't face consuming any form of bun or cake. My brother, Tony, called in on his way back from a police conference, and Lucy's sisters, Caroline and Jo, visited.

After a few days, a bed became available on one of the respiratory wards, and I was moved out of the office to a ward of six. The infection was not yet under control, and they had tried via trial and error a number of different antibiotics as the tests had come back as inconclusive with regard to the source pathogen. They weren't sure if it was viral, bacterial or fungal and checked for Legionnaires, and even HIV, in an attempt to figure out what they were dealing with, but the infection markers in the blood just continued to go up.

There was some talk about me potentially needing surgery if the infection spread to the pleural cavity, and this would require me transferring to a specialist unit, ironically back at UCH. This was alarming as it would be likely that there would be long-term consequences on lung function, and I was still at the stage of hoping that once the infection was under control, there would be a full recovery.

Finally, after what seemed like weeks, but was probably about 5 days, the infection markers seemed to stabilise. By this stage, I had a lot of fluid that needed draining from one of the lungs, which had partially collapsed, and this was done with a long needle on the Sunday morning after I had been admitted the previous Monday. This made a significant difference and probably marked the point at which I started to slowly feel better. I was keen to try and get out of bed, so I started a morning routine of some intervals up and down the ward, walking about 10 metres, past the area where the staff had their morning meeting. I think they thought I was completely mad and several asked what I was doing, to which I replied, 'training'.

The magnitude of what I was going through was brought home to me the following day during a visit by the respiratory consultant, Matthew Knight, on his morning rounds. I explained how much better I was feeling following the procedure to reinflate my lung by draining the fluid, and how I was looking forward to going home and resuming training as I had a world championships to prepare for in August[15].

He looked at me as if I were an utter idiot and told me that I wouldn't be training again for at least 6 months, and it would probably be 12 months before I could train again at the level I was familiar with. He explained that the infection had been very serious and would have impacted every organ in my body, summarising with the unforgettable conclusion that 'I had been hit by the biological equivalent of a bus'.

I was crushed, and when Luce arrived during visiting hours later that afternoon, I recounted Mr Knight's view and said we should just cancel the trips and races planned for 2017, including a return to Alpe d'Huez in July and Canada at the end of August.

Not for the first, or last, time in my life, I am thankful for Lucy's calm and logical mind in such situations, who replied saying 'well, let's not cancel anything at the moment and just see how things go'. These words proved to be wise and prophetic.

Although the infection markers were still way above the levels that

---

[15] I had entered the Long Distance World Champs for the first time, 3k swim, 120k bike and 30k run, to be held in Penticton, Western Canada

a normal, healthy person has[16], I was finally off the IV antibiotics, and the levels were now falling, so I could be discharged with oral antibiotics to hopefully finish the infection off over time. They hadn't found the infection source, and I was told by Mr Knight that I had simply been unlucky, but after 8 days, I was finally discharged and headed home. The time on the ward had been eye-opening, especially the way in which some people treat the staff who are there to care for them.

One guy was particularly odious, incredibly rude and obnoxious, swearing at and racially abusing nurses every day I was there. As I was leaving the ward and I was saying my goodbyes to my fellow patients, I had some choice words for this particular individual, which left him a little shocked. It never ceases to surprise me just how unpleasant some humans can be and how they never fail to disappoint. The care I had received, under very difficult circumstances, was fantastic, and I was, and will always be, very grateful to the staff at Watford Hospital who looked after me.

A couple of days later, I was sitting on a bench in Verulamium Park in St Albans, just enjoying the sun on my face, when my mobile rang. It was one of the registrars who had looked after me, to let me know the latest blood test results and that all they now wanted me to do was finish the antibiotics I had been discharged with. I asked about the next few weeks and he advised that in terms of exercise I should start with short, say 5-10 minute, walks. Great, I said, I'll do that, and what comes next, will I then be able to get back on my bike? The chap laughed at me, and just said, No, then

---

[16] Upon discharge my CRP marker was 46 mg/L, when a normal level is less than 5 mg/L. The infection peaked at 153 the previous week!

you can do some slightly longer walks. I was told to be careful, as if I wasn't, I'd be back in the hospital.

I was careful. The recovery road was going to be long and slow, but I was so happy to be out of hospital. I was surprisingly ok with the long road ahead and started preparing a plan. By the following week, when I had more bloods done and chest x-rays, the breathlessness had improved, and I was finally starting to sleep a bit better.

On April 4th I received the all clear; the x-ray showed some scarring, but this may not be permanent, and the blood results were good with the infection marker finally back to normal levels. I was ecstatic and celebrated with a 15-minute very easy spin on the Wattbike, vowing to never take any training session or race for granted ever again. I was very cautious over the next few weeks, gradually introducing and then building swim, bike and finally running.

Progress wasn't linear; there were definitely some bad days in there where I felt I'd never be fit again, but I started slowly to feel more and more like my old self. Grafman was cancelled in May, but I was already progressing rapidly by then, doing an hour FTP test on the bike on May 17th and averaging 292 watts. I was stoked, only 6 weeks after the all clear, and in significantly less time than predicted by Mr Knight, I was training at a decent level, at least on the bike. The run would take longer, but motivation levels were very high as I could see and feel the progress each week.

With the faster-than-expected return to training, Luce and I had a chat and decided to take a last-minute entry to the St Albans Half Marathon on 11th June. It was an emotional finish, with gratitude washing over me as I crossed the line in just over 90 minutes, a result which I could scarcely believe given where I had been only 2 months ago.

Fitness was progressing well, producing 310 watts for an hour by the end of June, and we decided to go ahead with the trip to the Alps for a return visit to the Alpe d'Huez triathlon. Probably not the ideal comeback race, and far from Mr Knight's recovery plan, but we were looking forward to the holiday with Matt and Katie so thought sod it, lets give it a go. First up was Long Course Weekend at Tenby in early July, which went really well and was a great weekend, providing some confidence for the Alps later in July.

We drove down to the Alps on the 15th July, with the plan to spend the first week enjoying riding from a base at Valloire before moving to Bourg d'Oisons the following week. Valloire was lovely, sitting at the top of the Col du Télégraphe, and at the bottom of the Col du Galibier, which meant there wasn't much flat around.

Every ride started either a descent or an ascent, and there were several attempts on the Galibier that week, including a PB on the climb. We had a lovely week in the sunshine, and I felt like I was still getting fitter every day, and feeling very grateful for it. The following Saturday, I rode over to Bourg, whilst Luce drove, to meet Matt and Katie. Riding our bikes in the Alps, preferably in the sunshine, is definitely one of our happy places, and we had a lovely holiday leading up the race, scheduled for Thursday, July 27th.

I had no expectations given that I was only getting discharged from hospital 4 months prior to race day, although I still had some nerves that morning, largely due to the fact that I just didn't know how I was going to hold up, especially in the latter stages. The weather was glorious, typically chilly first thing, which always makes the Alpe swim a challenge, but I was soon heading down the fast first section of the bike course, pedalling hard to try to warm up. I felt pretty good for most of the ride, although I did blow up a bit on the last section climbing Alpe d'Huez, and was relieved to stagger into T2.

The run was tough, and I started to suffer from hamstring cramps on the final lap when Matt caught me up and we ran down the finishing chute together, which seemed like a marvellous way to end the day. I'd finished 6th in my age group in 7 hours 16 minutes, but it wasn't about that at all. The emotions of the last few months came to a head at the finish line, leaving me feeling happy, grateful, surprised and relieved at completing such an epic race so soon after being hit by the biological equivalent of a bus.

Attention now turned to the Long Course World Championships, due to be held in Penticton in Western Canada at the end of August. I hadn't done these championships before, but I was excited to attempt the new distance, comprised of a 3km swim, 120km bike and 30km run. To qualify, you had to submit your best long-distance, or Ironman, race time to British Triathlon, and places were allocated to those who finished closest to the age group winner of that particular race. I hadn't done an Ironman, so I supplied my best half-ironman, or middle-distance, time and I was allocated a discretionary place given that the team wasn't full.

We flew to Vancouver on August 19th, hired a car and drove over the Rockies to Penticton. It was a beautiful location, with a crystal clear lake surrounded by mountains, and we had a lovely week leading up to the race the following weekend. Again, I had absolutely zero expectations and was simply very happy to be able to be there and preparing to stand on the start line, so the pressure was off. There were the normal butterflies in the stomach on race morning, but I'd recently read an insightful quote saying that such butterflies are good, you just need to ensure they are all flying in the same direction.

The swim went well, coming into T1 in 9th place in the age group to meet some epic wetsuit strippers, who shouted at me to 'lie down', which I meekly complied with. Two large Canadian guys then took one leg each and ripped my wetsuit off me, a new experience for me, resulting in probably my fastest transition to date. I headed off on the bike like a madman, with a race strategy to ride the bike leg as if it were a half ironman (I didn't have a power meter on my bike at this point and raced to feel), overtaking several guys in my AG within the first flat 40km section along the lake. I was having a blast and loving riding my bike as fast as I could in the sunshine through the stunning Western Canadian scenery.

I came into T2 and saw Luce holding her hand up with two fingers, which weren't abusing me, but indicating that I was in second place. I couldn't believe it and took off on the run, which was 3 laps around the town of Penticton, and soon overtook the guy to take the lead. As I came back round at the end of the first lap, I said to Luce that I couldn't quite believe what was happening as I was leading the world championships. Luce replied, 'Not for long', which quickly dispelled my exuberance as I knew it was a strong field, including a very fast runner and an ex-Canadian professional.

It wasn't long before the very fast American guy came cruising by me, but my head didn't go down; I was still in a podium position against what felt like all the odds. The temperature had risen considerably by now, and the heat off the tarmac and concrete sidewalks made the town feel like a furnace. I knew I was slowing, and I knew there were a couple of Canadian guys chasing me down, one of whom was the ex-pro, so the last few kilometres felt a lot longer than they were, but I managed to cling on, just, for the silver medal. I was ecstatic, again. A silver medal in my age group at a world championships, almost exactly 5 months since my discharge from Watford General.

Our Canadian trip had been joyous, a lovely place, a great race, and an opportunity to catch up with friends, as Jack (who Alex had introduced us to in Austria in 2016) was also racing, and also got on the podium, winning silver in the 20-24 age group. We met his parents, Mel and Paul, for the first time in Penticton and have remained good friends since.

I sent a postcard to the Respiratory Ward at the hospital, thanking them again for everything they did for me, but also to update them on my progress and result in Penticton. From the dark days of March, the 2017 season had delivered a performance and result, I could never have imagined. I remember leaving hospital with a determination to become fit again, I just wasn't sure how fit and in what timeframe, but I put a plan together and executed it to the best of my ability, never giving up when some days were distinctly average or painful, and just executing every session with whatever I had on the day. Achieving a podium position at an age group world championship meant that the goalposts now moved again, with the dream now evolving to finally, maybe, just maybe, one day standing on the top step at a world championship. I was due to turn 50 in 2018, so it felt like an appropriate time to dream big, although I would also be happy if I only managed to secure the top step in the 70-74 age group.

Lessons: never give up, fairytales can come true.

Modelling my first GB trisuit with my first TT bike, Spring 2008

GB team photo at my first age group experience, European Championships, Lisbon, May 2008. I'm hiding at the back somewhere together with my imposter syndrome

The support team at the 2013 World Championships in Hyde Park, London, September 2013. The largest and loudest supporter group I ever had at any race, shame I let them down on the day!

Winning gold at the European Championships, Rimini, Italy, May 2015. My first age group international win and another opportunity to move the goalposts

*Zell am See, Austria, September 2015, the setting for my first
Ironman 70.3 World Championships and one of the most
beautiful places I've raced at*

The finishing chute at Alpe D'Huez Triathlon with Matt, the comeback race after pneumonia, and hence the emotion, July 2017

Having fun riding my bike, Long Course World Champs, Penticton, Canada, August 2017

Celebrating with Jack at the finish in Penticton, 4 months after getting hit by a biological bus, August 2017

Grief

If 2017 proved to be a challenging year, then life was going to change irrevocably in 2018 and mark the start of a period of our lives which we were wholly unprepared for. Wrapping up 2017 first, I had one last race scheduled that year, the Ironman 70.3 in Weymouth in September, which would prove an opportunity to catch up with my brother, Tony, and his family, who lived in nearby Dorchester. Mum and Dad were also going to be there that weekend, and I was hoping to finish off the season in style and hopefully grab a slot for next year's 70.3 world championships, scheduled to be held in Port Elizabeth in South Africa.

Weymouth didn't go as planned. Starting with the weather, which was wet, windy and cold, resulting in a challenging swim. By the time I was running into T1, the rain was lashing down, and I exited transition like a drowned rat. Knowing I suffer from the cold, I rode off hard on the bike to try and warm up, and it seemed to be ok until about 10 miles in when I punctured.

My hands were cold, so trying to get the tyre off and a new tube in proved tricky with numb fingers, and it took about 10 minutes to get going again, by which time I had become significantly colder. We'd read reports that not all of the local community were that chuffed with the race happening, and there were rumours of diesel and tacks being thrown on the road that morning.

As an aside, I find this sort of stuff very sad and a tad depressing. Events are well publicised and I recognise that a little disruption may be experienced for a few hours, but with advance notice, I would have thought it would generally be possible to plan around it. It seems to be increasingly difficult to host events in the UK, especially those that may involve closing any roads temporarily, with the increasing venom and influence of keyboard warriors in our polarised society. Sad.

Anyway, back to a wet Dorset and about another 5 miles down a country lane, and another rear flat occurred. I did have another tube and CO2 cylinder, but the cylinder failed due to user error and even number fingers, and my race was over. I had to wait to get picked up by a broom wagon, which took a fair while, and I was very grateful to the race official on a motorbike who waited with me with his engine running, allowing me to try to stay warm in the vent of his exhaust. I eventually made it back to transition, cold, wet and miserable, chalking up my 3rd DNF. The plan to go to South Africa would need to be reworked.

The reworked plan involved a hastily planned return to Dubai in January 2018 to try to nab a qualifying slot. The race went well, clocking 4:20 overall and coming 2nd to Marcel Hotz, a Swiss guy whom I'd raced a few times (including lapping me on the run at Wiesbaden in 2016), and like Olaf, I'd never beaten. I came off the bike in the lead and was waiting for Marcel to catch me on the run, which subsequently happened with about 10km to go. I did manage to say, as he cruised by, 'Hi Marcel, I've been expecting you', to which he responded with 'yes, but you are so strong on zee bike'. Even though I have always lost to Marcel, I enjoy sharing the race course with him, a lovely guy, humble and very talented.

With the slot for South Africa acquired, I could focus on the rest of the season, which was designed with two peaks in mind: a return to the Long Course World Championships, this year in Fyn,

Denmark, in mid-July and the Ironman 70.3 World Championships in South Africa in September. With the result in Penticton, and a new age group to compete in, motivation was high to try to improve upon previous results at both events. Work was also extremely busy, and the potential acquisition of our company was now in full swing, with the various suitors whittled down to the large US bank, State Street, which commenced due diligence that spring.

Founding and building a business was hard work and stressful, but selling it was probably even more so, especially the pressure of making the right decisions for the team, the people who had left good careers at prestigious institutions to join us on this risky and mad journey. It was crazy that just over two years from founding BestX, we were commencing due diligence with a potential acquirer, but at the time, it just seemed a natural next step in the story.

I had a couple of domestic races before heading to Denmark; a return to Grafman and then the 113 Middle Distance Race in the Cotswolds, which provided an opportunity to also stay with Lucy's Mum and Dad, who lived in Cheltenham. Both races went well, winning my age group at both, coming 12th and 10th overall. I was riding well, averaging 289W and 275W at the two races, respectively, although my swim seemed to have plateaued, and I was stuck around the 30-minute mark for 1900m, at least in freshwater.

The 113 race came at the end of a week which I had spent away with work in Boston, getting grilled in some detail by teams of people at State Street as part of the due diligence process, so I was tired and stressed flying home on the Friday and was particularly pleased to have delivered a decent performance.

After this race I took some time to reflect and see what else I could do to be peaking for Denmark and noted down in my training diary that I needed to sort my swim out, try to cut out alcohol leading up to the race, maximise my sleep, try to squeeze a bit more run speed out and attempt to minimise work stress. The last of these was to prove impossible, but was well-intended.

In terms of abstinence from, for example, alcohol, I've never been one of those triathletes who religiously adhere to some regime or other and have always adopted a more relaxed policy of moderation.

Over the years, I've met numerous age groupers who, for example, try to cut out sugar, or only consume caffeine on race day, or totally abstain from alcohol, and none of them seem to have produced outstanding results. Each to their own, and yes, you could argue that I don't know what effect a more disciplined lifestyle would have had on my performances, but this is a hobby and I enjoy buns too much to care.

Preparation for Denmark had gone as well as could be expected given the work demands. I'd continued to optimise training as best I could, including, for example, arranging to hire a bike when on a work trip to Geneva to get a ride in the mountains with a client who also liked riding his bike. Probably the best work 'meeting' I ever had. We travelled over to Fyn on Wednesday, 11th July, with the race due to happen on the Saturday. I had the usual pre-race build-up, including a reconnaissance of the swim and bike course on the Thursday.

The former was full of jellyfish, and the latter was flat and windy. I felt like I was in decent shape and was excited to race against what looked like a strong start list of competitors, although in hindsight, the build-up did feel different to other major events.

Looking back, I was undoubtedly somewhat distracted, and stressed, not helped by having a long work call on the Friday afternoon before the race where it had become apparent that there was a potential spanner in the works with regards to the sale of BestX and there was a risk that the deal may fall through. After months of working on the sale of the business, the thought that it may not happen now wasn't ideal, and it certainly wasn't ideal race preparation.

My swim with the jellyfish was disappointing, although other people's GPS files indicated it may have been a little over the 3km (I don't wear a watch, so I wasn't sure), coming out in 13th place. I had a great ride to help make amends, averaging 278W over the 120km and working my way up the field. I wasn't aware how far in front the leaders were, but I stuck to the task at hand and set out onto the 3-lap run course. It took a while to get going, seemed to have a purple patch in the middle lap, and then slowed considerably on the last lap.

I ended up coming 5th in the age group, which I was disappointed with, especially given it was my first year in the 50-54 age group and on a course which, in theory, should have suited me. I now look back at this race, and the disappointment is mitigated by the fact that I was obviously very stressed with work at the time, and I have no doubt that extrinsic stresses like work can have a significant impact on athletic performance.

I think the authors Steve Magness and Brad Stulberg once wrote that you should allow yourself 24 hours after any result, good or bad, to either celebrate or wallow, and then you move on and get back to work. Wise words that I have tried to adopt in practice, and we headed back to London on the Sunday with a mid-season break ahead of me to provide time to recharge physically and mentally.

In early August, we celebrated our silver wedding anniversary with a party at our house for family and friends. Unbeknownst to us at the time, it would be the last time that our four parents would be together.

Lucy's Mum, Kate, had been unwell for a while, with uncertainty around a specific diagnosis, other than that she was very tired and struggling to eat. I think at some point that summer pancreatitis was put forward as a potential cause of her symptoms, and she was admitted to Cheltenham General later in August, mainly to help ensure that she was consuming sufficient calories. We were due to fly to South Africa for the 70.3 world championships on the 25th and travelled back to Cheltenham the week before to visit Kate in hospital. Kate urged us to go to South Africa, and there was no indication of what was to come at all. I still remember her leaving the chair by her bed to say goodbye in the lift lobby, squeezing my arm affectionately in the way she had done ever since first meeting her in 1991.

We decided on the drive home along the A40 to still go away. We were worried about Kate and uncertain that a full and accurate diagnosis had been made, but she was in good hands in the hospital, and her spirits were seemingly good. The issues with the BestX sale had been resolved, due diligence had been completed, and the final paperwork was with the lawyers and wasn't due to be signed until we returned. So, we flew on the 25th as planned, hired a car and drove over to Port Elizabeth, stopping at a couple of locations on the way.

We arrived in the race venue on the Wednesday, built the bike and screwed up by trapping the gear cable in the headset, resulting in a bit of a flap to find a mechanic to replace the cable. Once resolved, I did the usual course reconnaissance on Thursday and was feeling ready.

The swim was notoriously tough due to the swell, as strong winds in Port Elizabeth at this time of year were common, and the forecast for race day wasn't great; windy and wet. I bought myself a rain jacket for the bike, really to try to stay warm as I had enough experience in wet and cold conditions by now, but I hoped it wouldn't be needed. I can't remember exactly what day that week, but we were made aware that Kate had been discharged from hospital, which we assumed was a good thing. However, the situation remained fluid and uncertain, and discussions with family on the Saturday were worrying as it became increasingly clear that she should probably be readmitted.

After a very poor night's sleep on the Saturday, worrying about home, race day dawned, and I rolled out of bed to find some strange marks on my abdomen. I didn't really think twice about them and assumed they were due to bed bugs, as the Airbnb we were staying at wasn't the most salubrious. The weather was as forecast, with high winds and dark, foreboding skies looming overhead as we headed down to transition, bumping into Marcel and his partner on the way.

The ocean looked pretty angry with a heavy swell, and it was with some trepidation that I ran into it off the beach. It was a challenging swim, although I had a surprisingly good one, coming out in the top 10% in my age group in just over 29 minutes. I took the decision to put on a rain jacket in transition as it was cold and starting to rain, but I regretted it later. It wasn't a particularly aero jacket and flapped about in the wind, undoubtedly costing me time on the bike, but at least I don't remember getting cold. It was a disappointing bike split, 18th in the age group when I would normally expect to place much higher, but as always, I was grateful to arrive back in transition with no mechanicals or punctures[17] , and the usual thought flashed through my mind, 'at least I will now be able to finish'.

The run was two laps, with hills at either end of the course, and I ran off determined to try to move up the placings. I had a great run, probably one of the best I've ever had, clocking just over 1:25 with little fade in the second half, which was particularly unusual for me. This was the 7th fastest run split and had moved me up to 7th overall in the 50-54 category, one place better than the last time I competed at these championships in Zell three years ago.

The pro race was also a classic, coming down to a 3-way run battle between Ali Brownlee, Javier Gomez and Jan Frodeno, and is often now referred to as one of the greatest middle distance races of all time. As I made it through the finish area, with the rain coming down, I could see Luce on her phone, getting updates from back home, and looking very worried. The decision had been taken for Kate to go back into hospital as she wasn't eating at home and

---

[17] I had sadly seen Marcel at the side of the road with a mechanical

was in considerable pain and discomfort.

We headed back to our accommodation with thoughts fully focused on Kate. We were due to stay in South Africa another week for a holiday, and the advice from home that day was that the hospital readmittance was precautionary, and we should finish off our holiday.

Luckily, we decided to pack the bike up that afternoon, a job which is always hard to get round to immediately post-race when you are tired, both physically and cognitively, and collapsed into bed for an early night. We were woken in the night, I think around 3 am, with a call from Lucy's sister, phoning to inform us of the heartbreaking news that Kate had died in hospital that night. We were utterly shocked. We knew Kate wasn't well, but we had absolutely no idea that this was imminent, and the news hit us like a thunderbolt.

After the initial shock, we switched to autopilot, realising immediately that we needed to get back to the UK as soon as possible, so we quickly got up, packed our remaining belongings and threw everything in the back of the car. A storm had rolled in by now, and we left Port Elizabeth, tears rolling down our faces, in the early hours of the morning, with the rain lashing down to commence the long drive back to Cape Town.

Not long after dawn, we stopped off at a café for a toilet break and coffee, still very much in shock. Sitting down at the table, the waitress came over, saw our faces, and sweetly asked if we were ok. We both simply burst into tears and tried to briefly explain, which probably wasn't the response she was expecting, and I got the distinct feeling she'd regretted asking us. We were back on the road quickly, constantly phoning British Airways to try and get our flight booking rearranged as we'd headed off to Cape Town without a flight to board. Luckily, we were able to get seats on the flight later that day, although not sitting together, which was far from ideal, but we thought we'd try to resolve that once we arrived at check-in.

After what seemed like an eternity, we finally arrived at Cape Town airport, not paying huge attention to speed limits on the way,[18] and went to check in for the overnight flight. Another emotional breakdown, and we finally managed to get seats together upon boarding the flight, although neither of us slept, and we lay there in the dark waiting to land at Heathrow.

Lucy's family had gathered at Gloucester Royal Hospital on the Monday morning, and our plan was therefore to head home to St Albans upon landing to drop off the luggage, repack a bag, have a shower, pick up the car and drive directly to the hospital. In hindsight, this was probably a mistake, and we should have taken a little more time and then gone to see Kate on our own, in our own time, rather than as part of a large family group.

Arriving at the hospital I remember greeting Lucy's Dad, Paddy, telling him how sorry I was, to which he responded with 'yes, bit of a bugger really'. Everyone was in shock, and the memories of that day will always remain with us. We'd both experienced grief, with the death of grandparents, aunts and uncles, but nothing prepares you for the loss of a parent. Western culture seems to be poor at talking about death and trying to prepare people for the

---

[18] Over the next few weeks we received numerous letters from South Africa informing us of speeding tickets that day, I think we ended up with 6 or 7.

inevitability of it, and there is no hyperbole in saying that life utterly changed that day.

The days that followed seem quite blurred now, a mixture of shock, grief and sadness with the practicalities of dealing with the next steps and arranging a funeral. On Wednesday, I noticed that the rash that I'd first noticed in Port Elizabeth on Sunday morning had developed and was now spreading up the side of my abdomen in an arc.

With everything else that was going on, I managed to get an out-of-hours GP appointment in the evening at Cheltenham hospital, to be told that I had shingles. This was a surprise, to say the least, and given my age and the fact that it had now been longer than 48 hours since the rash first appeared, I wasn't eligible for the normally prescribed anti-virals.

As it turned out, I was very lucky and only had a mild dose, as no further symptoms developed and the rash started to go within a couple of weeks, but I did wonder if it would have had any impact on race day, which now seemed like an age away.

In the meantime, the sale of BestX was completed on September 11th as I flew with Ollie to Barcelona for a conference. With everything else that had happened, this major event seemed to pass me by a little, but it was another life-changing moment. It did mean that I wouldn't have to work again if I didn't want to, providing Lucy and I with the flexibility and freedom to do whatever we wanted.

However, as is common in such transactions, the sale did require us to remain working, still for BestX, but as part of the acquiring company, State Street, for three years. This would prove to be quite a culture shock, from founding a small company, surrounded by high-calibre, driven individuals, to becoming a cog in a large corporate institution again, with multiple layers of management and considerable bureaucracy. There were whispers in the market, some of which were not so whispery, that we had 'sold out and taken the money and run', and yes, of course, the deal was financially beneficial to all of us, but a larger component in the decision was to try to ensure longevity for the business and brand.

Our costs, especially those for market data, were rising significantly, our clients were demanding that we expand our product range, and we were very conscious that long-term survival was going to require the firepower of a large institution. State Street offered this security, and as I write in 2025, almost 7 years since the acquisition, the product and brand are still going strong.

Kate's funeral took place on Monday, September 17th, on a bright, sunny, early autumnal day in Cheltenham, at the church where we were married in 1991. A terribly sad day, but also the opportunity to remember a lovely person, one of the warmest, most caring and selfless people I have ever met. She made me very welcome from the first moment I met her, and I miss her, especially the times in the kitchen after a meal whilst washing up, or seeing her sitting on the bench with a coffee whilst I cut the hedge.

There were two races left in the calendar for 2018, and Lucy and I had a few conversations about whether to go ahead with them and whether our hearts were in it. In the end we decided to go ahead, with the first trip due to be a long weekend away in Cascais, Portugal, just north of Lisbon for the Ironman 70.3 race, where the original plan had been to try to grab a qualifying slot for the following year's world championship, to be held in Nice.

Training had obviously taken a back seat for a while, but we thought the trip may actually help a little, so we flew out to Lisbon late on the Thursday evening before the race. We loved Cascais, a really lovely town with a very relaxed feel, and we were glad to be away, and the race went well. I ended up coming second in the age group, with a decent swim of just under 30 minutes, a strong bike split and an adequate run of 1:31 on a pretty lumpy course. The slot for Nice was taken, and we headed back to London on Monday morning.

The last race of the season was the European Middle Distance Championships, this year being held in Ibiza at the end of October. Lucy's sisters, Caxster and Rachel, joined us for the trip, and we spent a long weekend enjoying the sunshine, apart from on race day. Race day morning was dreadful, very heavy rain with thunderstorms and high winds, and the race organisers had to delay the start until at least the lightning had finished. This meant the start getting delayed until mid-afternoon, at which time they had to also cut the bike course short as otherwise athletes would be riding in the dark. It wasn't ideal, with the uncertainty around the start time making pre-race nutrition very challenging and certainly sub-optimal as I would discover later on the run.

The rain was still coming down but the thunderstorms had passed so we headed off on the swim into a pretty angry Mediterranean. Strangely, I had a good swim, coming out 2nd in the age group with only my old nemesis, Olaf, ahead of me. The rain came down heavier on the bike and large amounts of surface water made the course tricky, not aided by the temperatures as once again I got very cold on the bike and struggled to put power down or control the bike due to shivering.

I lost some places on the bike, an occurrence I wasn't used to, but tried to make the best of it on the run. The delayed start and inappropriate pre-race fuelling started to haunt me with some major GI distress occurring as the run went on, so I was very relieved to finish, crossing the line and heading straight to a portaloo without stopping, closely resembling Forrest Gump. Somehow, I'd managed to sneak onto the podium and grab a bronze medal, with Olaf taking gold again and extending his lead to 5-0.

I was due to turn 50 in December and we spent some time earlier in the year discussing how to celebrate. Luce asked me if I could do anything at all on my 50th birthday what would I do, and I replied 'I'd love to race'. As chance would have it, Ironman announced their inaugural La Quinta 70.3 race that year, to be held in southern California on my actual birthday. Perfect we thought, the stars have aligned, and we happily booked the trip.

Events, however, conspired against us as that autumn my Dad was diagnosed with a large abdominal aortic aneurysm, which was going to require pretty urgent and major surgery. Sometime in November we received the news that the surgery had been booked in, for Monday December 10th, the day after my birthday race day.

My parents were obviously very worried about the procedure, which was going to require several hours of surgery with a significant risk of complications, and it was clear that my Mum was going to need looking after that day, and afterwards, whilst Dad recovered in hospital. We felt like we had no choice but to cancel the California trip and head to a wet North Wales instead for a very different 50th birthday celebration than I had anticipated. In hindsight it was a good job we changed our plans as on the Monday, whilst Dad was in theatre, my Mum had a panic attack and we were there, at least, to help her. Thankfully, the operation went well and I stayed with Mum for the remainder of the week to help with other complex life issues, such as turning the TV on and explaining how to use a mobile phone. Mum wasn't one for technology, of any form.

2018 had been a life-changing year and it taught me that you should never take anyone or anything for granted as they can be taken away from you in the blink of an eye. Pneumonia had taught me that when it comes to health, training and racing but the unexpected death of Kate had brought this home when it comes to those that you love.

Lessons: don't take anybody or anything for granted.

A rare photo of me running with feet off the ground at a wet 70.3 world champs in Port Elizabeth, South Africa, September 2018

The swim start at Cascais, Portugal, September 2018, another of our favourite race locations

Another defeat to Olaf, this time at the European Middle Distance Champs, Romania, July 2019, making the scoreline a rather humiliating Olaf 6, Pete 0, but I was getting closer!

On my way to another silver medal at the Long Course World Champs, Pontevedra, Spain, May 2019

Chasing Olaf into a mega headwind, Samorin, Slovakia, August 2022

125

A very emotional finish at the 'Long' Course World Champs,
Samorin, Slovakia, August 2022

Finally, a world championship age group title, but more importantly, at the 7th attempt, on the step above Olaf, X-Bionic Sphere, Slovakia, August 2022

Having fun at Outlaw Holkam, July 2023, photo courtesy of Two26 Photography and, specifically, Jack's Dad, Paul

Swim start, Long Course World Champs, Ibiza, May 2023,
another photo courtesy of Paul, Two26 Photography

At the finish with friends and family, after escaping the clutches of a couple of weaping, sweaty Italians, Ibiza, May 2023

The day after Ironman Austria, one and done and finally a proper triathlete, June 2024

Chasing Mark Clough, Long Distance World Champs,
Townsville, August 2024

Remembering our parents at the finish of the Long Course World Champs, August 2024

Having fun and trying to be the best I can be is My Why, Ironman 70.3 World Champs, Taupo, New Zealand, December 2024

Persistence

The commute to Canary Wharf returned in 2019 following the acquisition as we had to relocate to work out of our new owner's offices, which I found as palatable as scooping out my eyeballs with rusty spoons but needs must. By not racing for my 50th, the end-of season break had lasted for 2-3 weeks in December, but I was raring to go again with training by the beginning of the year.

I often retest to check where I'm at as I enter a new training phase, principally just to ensure my zones are appropriate, and looking back at the training diary shows I knocked out 344 watts for 20 minutes on January 9th, which I was chuffed with as it indicated I was heading into the year already in decent shape. I also did a day at the Boardman Performance Centre, sadly no longer in operation, on the 19th of January for more testing on the bike, including determining my lactate thresholds, but just as importantly, substrate consumption at different training intensities.

I was planning to return to the Long Distance World Championships to try to improve upon the disappointing performance the previous year in Denmark, and I wanted to get more scientific on the fuelling requirements for these longer distance races. For example, it was important to determine what power and heart rate levels corresponded to the points where I was still largely consuming fat as fuel. The swim and run were in ok shape, I was uninjured, and I was motivated for the year ahead.

The season kicked off in mid-April in Greece at the inaugural Ironman 70.3, on the coast approximately 2 hours drive west of Athens. We planned a holiday around the race again, with the trip including a couple of days in Athens after the race. As often seems to be the case, race day dawned with terrible weather, dark threatening skies and very high winds, which resulted in probably the most stressful swim I've ever had.

Nowadays, I'm pretty certain that Ironman would have cancelled the swim given the roughness of the sea, but back in 2019, we ran off the beach into the largest breakers I've ever swum in. It was almost impossible to sight, not helped by my goggles getting knocked off by the power of the waves.

As we turned back towards the beach, before another turn running parallel with the beach to the swim exit, I could see lots of people simply heading straight onto the beach and running several hundred metres to the beach rather than completing the swim course. The relief at finally getting out of the water was enormous, but I knew as I was already a fair bit behind the front of the race, so I rode off on my bike like a madman.

The bike course was lumpy, windy and wet as the heavens opened, but I rode ok, producing a normalised power of 290W and riding into second place. Another nemesis of mine, Graham Baxter, who I'd come second to at Cascais the previous year and was a monster on the bike, was a fair way down the road, but you just never know what can happen, especially in longer distance races, so I've always adopted the attitude of never give up. I had a good run on a beautiful course around a nature reserve, finishing with a 1:28, which was the fastest run split in the age group and secured my second position.

I was pleased with the early season performance, particularly the bike and run, and we headed off to Athens the following morning in high spirits until I quickly fell ill on the drive and had to spend the day in bed with nausea, fever and chills. Luckily, it only lasted 24 hours, and we managed to see the sights over the following couple of days. We had a great time in the sunshine.

In January, I made the decision to start working with Matt Bottrill Performance Coaching to try to improve my bike performance, in addition to continuing to work with Bill Black for the overall program. I met with Matt, who had a look through my training and discussed my rider profile before deciding to allocate me to one of his senior coaches, Simon Beldon. I clicked with Simon quickly, liking his no-bullshit, tough-love style of coaching, coupled with a very deep knowledge and scientific basis. The bike split in Greece gave me some confidence that the plan was working.

The world champs were only just around the corner on 4th May, hence the reason to find an early season race to blow the cobwebs away, and we headed off to Northern Spain at the end of April. There were other folks racing that we knew, including Jack (who had also raced Penticton and Fyn), and it was good catching up. We also met Vic, Jack's new girlfriend, for the first time and had a lovely few days enjoying Pontevedra. Triathlon had once again brought us somewhere that we would never have visited, and we really enjoyed exploring, managing to find the time for a day in Porto on the way home.

As it was early in the year, water temperatures were still chilly, so the 3 km swim was shortened to approximately 1.5 km, which suited me just fine. We'd observed the river prior to race day and noticed how strong the current was and devised a strategy to try to make the most of it, which worked well as I came out of the water in 3rd place in my age group, a feat that I wouldn't ever repeat at a world championships!

The bike was lumpy, with some technical sections, and although my descending skills still let me down a bit, I had a good ride, producing a normalised power of 280 watts and riding into T2 in 3rd place in my age group. I was desperate to perform better than the 5th place in Denmark and started out on the run in a positive state of mind, quickly catching the guy in second and trying to stay focused on fuelling and hydrating. I wasn't closing the gap on the leader but stuck to the task in hand, but annoyingly, cramp hit both hamstrings in the last kilometre, and I had to walk a couple of times to try to stretch it out.

Thankfully, the gap to third was large enough to accommodate this, and I crossed the line with another silver medal at a world championship.

I met the winner, Arnaud Selukov, at the medal ceremony, who said to me that his dream was always to win a world championships in his age group when he was 50, which resonated with me. Seeing him with his kids, clearly very emotional as he absorbed achieving his goal, fuelled my fire to go one better next year. Two silver medals were great, and I was pleased with my performance, but as someone once said, second place is really only the first loser.

Next up was the British Middle Distance Championships, this year to be held in Chester as part of the Deva Triathlon in early June. I recovered from Pontevedra quickly and was excited to race, especially as the location had fond memories for me, providing my qualification spot for the 2013 Olympic distance world champs with a very unexpected age group win. Mum and Dad drove over from North Wales to watch, unbeknown to me at the time that this would be the last time my Mum would see me compete. Mum was aware of the second places at the world championships and often used to say to me that she just knew that one day I'd be a world champion, with absolutely no idea of what was involved in achieving that goal, but it was very sweet for her to have such complete faith in me.

Deva was a great event, I loved it. Another river swim with a strong current, so Luce and I did our homework on the Saturday and planned a strategy, which once again worked well, coming out of the water in 4th place in the age group after finding and staying on some feet for the upstream section of the course. I always find it very hard to find feet to swim on, the ones around me always seem either too fast or too slow, so this was a novelty that I quite enjoyed. The bike was marvellous fun, again pushing out 290 watts and quickly riding into first place. It was during this event that I started to race with a disc wheel for the first time, and it felt and sounded great.

On the run, Luce let me know I had a decent gap, so I didn't have to run off like a loon, which was music to my ears as I was a little worried I may have overcooked it on the bike. One of the guys behind me was a fast runner, so I knew I couldn't just coast, but it was nice to have the pressure off to some extent, and I ran another 1:28 split to take the 50-54 national title in 4:13 overall. After two second places so far this year, it was satisfying to stand on the top step.

Aside from Pontevedra, the other A race for 2019 was the Ironman

70.3 world championships in Nice in September. I was aware that the bike course included a very long and technical descent, so I was keen to ride it in advance to decide whether to take a road or TT bike.

Luckily an opportunity presented itself as the week after Deva, I was due to present at a client conference in Nice, so I hired a road bike locally and rode the course. It was a beautiful ride, but I was under no illusions about how little it played to my strengths, so I started to mentally prepare for a proper schooling from the European uber-riders on how to descend a mountain on a bike, as I had witnessed a couple of times at the Alpe d'Huez race. Anyway, I decided I'd better take a road bike as I did not trust myself to get down the descent in one piece on my TT bike.

A return to the European Middle Distance Championships was on the calendar before Nice, this year due to be held in Targa Mures in Romania. This was a destination that we definitely wouldn't have travelled to if it wasn't for triathlon! That would have been a shame as it was a great trip, staying in a hotel that could have been designed for a Russian porn movie but in a lovely town. Even having to experience Whizz Air for the first time wasn't too traumatic.

Central Europe in July was hot, very hot, so it was clear that the swim was going to be non-wetsuit, which was going to make it even harder to finally get a score on the board in the multi-year battle with Olaf, who I had seen was on the start list.

The swim went better than I expected, coming out 4th in the age group, which was a result given the lack of a wetsuit. However, I'd still given up over 6 minutes to Olaf, so I had to put the hammer down on the 4-lap bike course. The bike was a blast, and I overtook Olaf sometime on the 3rd lap I think and tried to put as much time as possible into him for the remainder of the course. Olaf must have picked up the pace upon seeing me go by, as although I entered T2 in the lead, I could see Olaf not far behind me as I headed out on the run. Sure enough, after the first kilometre, I heard footsteps behind me and saw my nemesis run up alongside me with a brief nod of acknowledgement.

For the next 8 kilometres or so, we ran side by side, which was fantastic and felt like 'proper' racing. We didn't speak, probably because we were both trying to appear composed and cruising along, whereas the reality was that we were blowing out of our arses; well, I was. By now, it was even hotter and very humid as a thunderstorm looked to be brewing, and towards the halfway mark the elastic very gradually began to snap as Olaf started to move ahead of me.

For some time, I kept him in sight and desperately tried to close the gap, but I had nothing left and had to watch the gold medal disappear down the road. It was Groundhog Day; first loser again and 6-0 to Olaf. We had a chat at the finish, congratulating each other, and I pointed out that I was now of the opinion that I would never beat him. He sheepishly smiled and replied that he thought I would one day.

Upon returning from Romania, we completed on our house purchase in Cheltenham, with the long-term plan to move permanently once I had finished working my earn-out period at State Street. In the meantime, it would serve as a good base as Luce had gone part-time and was travelling over every week to help look after her Dad. It also provided an opportunity for me to incur a whole new injury to add to the litany of issues over the years; a torn glute muscle, achieved by trying to lug a very heavy mattress up the stairs. I sought physio treatment quickly, and biking was permitted as it didn't seem to cause any issues, but run training was going to be impacted, which wasn't ideal given the world champs in Nice were under 2 months away.

We were combining Nice with another holiday, driving down to Annecy for a week, which was one of our favourite places in the Alps, before heading on down to Nice via a couple of days at Ventoux. It was a glorious trip with lots of sunshine, good food, wine and riding, including a memorable day that we summitted Ventoux. Nice was also fantastic, and we fell in love with the city, thoroughly enjoying the weather and atmosphere and spending time with Jack and Alex, who had also both qualified. The race didn't go so well.

Another non-wetsuit swim (even though the day before for the women's race had been wetsuit legal) didn't kick the day off well, but I was used to this and was no longer phased by it. The bike course was stunning, but I quickly discovered that my choice of road bike was the wrong one, as folks went tearing by me on TT bikes on the beginning flat section. The climb up Col de Vence went ok, and I made up many places, moving up to 17th, only to lose them again, and many more, on the technical descent, as I had feared.

Watching some of these guys descend was pretty terrifying, and I heard after the race that Nice A&E was full of injured cyclists, so I was cautious and relieved to get back onto the flat section and back into the city. My biggest disappointment in my race performance was the run, which was a flat 2-lap course up and down the Promenade des Anglais.

The lack of run training over the summer obviously didn't help, but a 1:35, coupled with stomach cramps, wasn't what I would have hoped for. I ended up finishing in 46th place in my age group and was disappointed after finishing in the Top 10 on my two previous attempts at these championships. It was a long drive home the following day, with plenty to ruminate over, but I tried to stick to the 'give yourself 24 hours to either celebrate or wallow' rule as I had one more race in the 2019 season.

We were back in time to see my niece, Rosie, get married to Scott before we returned to Cascais with friends, including Matt and Katie, as we had loved it so much the previous year. The objective was to try and achieve some redemption following Nice, but more importantly, to try to qualify for next year's world championships, which were due to be held in New Zealand. If I qualified, the plan was to have a 'big trip,' combining the race with a three-week early retirement trip, so the pressure was on to get a slot.

It was another lovely long weekend, only arriving on the Friday before the race as I had been away with work in Boston and only arrived back in the UK on Thursday. The race went well, a good swim and bike put me in the lead, and I managed to hang on to the lead through a challenging, hot and lumpy run. Qualification and redemption were achieved, and it felt good to finish off the season, not on the second step of the podium. We could also start planning our New Zealand trip, with no idea of what was coming in 2020 to completely derail it.

The new year dawned, and we excitedly made our plans, including the end of year holiday to New Zealand, but kicking off first with a trip to Oman in February for the Ironman 70.3 in Muscat. We'd visited Oman a couple of times, and it was our favourite Middle Eastern destination, not having the bling and flashiness of Dubai and the other Emirates.

We were aware of the news coming out of China, but by the time we were due to go to Oman, no restrictions had been put in place, and I don't think anyone knew just how horrendous things were going to get. We discussed whether to still fly and decided to go, albeit masked up, but it was still quite a shock seeing everyone getting temperature screened at Muscat airport. Once in Muscat, there was no sign of the impending pandemic, and we temporarily pushed it to the back of our minds.

The race went well, with lovely calm conditions for the swim, but I was still shocked to clock a 27-minute swim, my best swim for many years. The bike course was great, although the lack of riding outside over the winter took its toll, especially on the climbs. I've never been one of these triathletes who advocates one or the other when it comes to the age-old debate of bike training indoors or outdoors. I've always done both, and I feel that a combination provides the best of both worlds, especially given I'm generally a fair-weather rider who doesn't particularly enjoy getting cold and wet.

At the end of the day, this is a hobby, and if the enjoyment is sucked out of it, then I should find another hobby. Yes, I'm aware of the argument that it is important to ride outside in all weathers as you never know what the conditions on race day will be like, but after many years competing, I feel like I've ridden on enough wet and windy race days to now have sufficient experience.

Anyway, it was a decent bike split, and it meant I ran out of transition in second place with a Russian guy somewhere down the road. I was pleased with the run, even with the usual fade, as 1:29 in hot conditions off a hard bike gave me the age group win and 8th overall, my highest-ever place in an Ironman event.

I was off again on a work trip to the US the day after we got home from holiday, and by this time, it was clear that life was going to change pretty quickly. I recall sitting at Baltimore airport on February 27th waiting for my flight, which had been delayed 8 hours, feeling very rough, which in hindsight was probably Covid as I didn't feel 'right' for the next 2 to 3 weeks. I took the decision to start working from home in early March, the swimming pools closed on March 17th, and we were then subjected to the first lockdown on March 24th, with outdoor exercise restricted to once per day.

Looking back now, it all feels like a very bad dream, but living through it at the time was a new and alarming experience. We quickly decided to move our plan forward and relocate to Cheltenham immediately, given that we were now fully working from home, which would then allow us to be close to Lucy's Dad to help out as required as part of the support bubble. It was also very clear that the 2020 triathlon season was going to be non-existent, and New Zealand were quick to close their borders putting an end to the planned December big trip for the world championships.

Training had to adjust, with swim cords replacing the pool time, at least until open-water swimming was possible. I did try a couple of virtual events that Ironman arranged and also ran a Spitfire remote 10km, clocking 38:53, which I was pleased with at 51. It has been a challenge dealing with slowing down with age, and a 10km time approximately 4 minutes slower than my PB was a bit depressing, but that is where both age grading and racing in 5-year bands helps to some extent.

I've tried to implement the various aspects of training that are widely promoted to help with age-based decline, including mobility and flexibility work, strength training and keeping some high-intensity work, although the latter has had to be carefully managed, especially on the run, given the increased injury risk. More recently, I've tried adopting the mantra that ageing is a privilege and having gratitude for the fact that I am still healthy enough to be able to exercise.

Life was about to take another twist. My parents had finally taken the decision to move from North Wales to somewhere nearer by, initially looking at Ross-on-Wye, before settling on a bungalow that Lucy found them in Cirencester, about 25 minutes from where we lived. That August, our offer on the property was accepted, and it was the happiest I'd seen my Mum in a very long time. I think she had really struggled through the early part of the pandemic and had found the lockdown particularly stressful.

When they visited in August, I was concerned about her health. She seemed to have lost more weight and was very frail. The difficulties in accessing healthcare during the pandemic hadn't helped at all as her heart was a concern, as were the couple of falls and blackouts that she'd had in preceding months. When she left us in August to drive back to North Wales, she stood in the drive and gave me the biggest hug I think she ever had and told me that she really loved me. This was very out of character, and I'm not sure it had ever happened before.

We were at Lucy's Dad's on Sunday, September 13th, and had just finished lunch with him when my mobile rang. In a very flustered and fairly incoherent manner, my Dad proceeded to tell me that Mum had 'had a funny turn' and was being taken to hospital. I tried to probe for more information but had to wait to speak to the hospital once she'd been admitted to determine the seriousness of her condition.

The A&E staff nurse told me that she was in a coma and had suffered a catastrophic bleed on the brain, and he suggested that I should make my way to the hospital as quickly as possible. I called my brother to give him the news and told him to head to Wales immediately, given he was in Dorchester and even further away than I was, before heading home to quickly pack a bag and start the drive to North Wales.

I arrived at A&E about 4 hours later to find Dad in a state of shock by Mum's bed. The staff nurse I'd spoken to on the phone came to meet me and took me to one side to explain that she would not recover, repeating the phrase 'catastrophic brain bleed' before I promptly threw up in a nearby sink. He said that it was unknown how long she would survive; it could be a few hours to days, but there should be no doubt about the ultimate outcome.

My brother and his wife arrived a couple of hours later, thankfully whilst Mum was still alive, together with my nephew and his girlfriend. I have no idea whether she could hear what was said to her, but I take some comfort in believing that she was aware, deep in her consciousness, that we were all there. Mum was moved from the A&E ward to a separate room to wait for the inevitable, which very sadly occurred at around 1 am when she passed away.

Watching your Mum die before your eyes is as traumatic as it sounds, and the initial grief was very raw. I have vague memories of howling like a dog at her bedside, not wanting to believe what had just happened. Mum and I were close, perhaps less so in latter years, and we had very different political views which had resulted in numerous heated arguments, but the bond had remained.

The memories from the following weeks are pretty blurred now through the fog of grief. I found grief a confusing and unexpected mix of emotions, including an anger that seemed to spring from nowhere. One morning, Luce and I were out running and about to cross a road. I looked over my shoulder and saw a car approaching, but it wasn't indicating and therefore assumed it wouldn't be turning into us.

As we ran across the road, the car turned into the road, narrowly missing us, with the driver screaming abuse through his window. The red mist descended, and I lost the plot, turning to give him both barrels. He made the mistake of stopping the car, and I headed over to drag him out of his open window. The guy went pale and started to try to hide behind the fact he had his kids in the back, even though he'd already sworn at us.

Fortunately, Luce was there to defuse the situation by pointing out that this wasn't a good idea as ending up in a police station on a GBH charge wouldn't be the smartest given Mum's funeral was in a couple of days. I'm not proud of it, but I just seemed to totally lose control and burst into tears on the side of the road as the guy drove off.

I largely remained in Wales to try to look after Dad, who was utterly bereft and inconsolable, whilst arranging the funeral. His entire life had revolved around Mum; she was his first girlfriend, and he had dedicated his life to looking after and providing for her. It was heartbreaking to witness his grief.

As a kid, I had always been a bit scared of Dad, he was a big guy and sometimes had a temper, so seeing him sobbing his heart out when I hadn't seen him cry before was distressing. Even though the lockdown had ended, we were still subject to Covid restrictions, so I wasn't allowed to help carry the coffin, and we were only allowed 15 mourners at the crematorium. I delivered the eulogy, only just holding it together, and vowed to myself that I would, one day, deliver on Mum's expectation that I would be an age group world champion.

I wasn't going to give up trying; I had no particular talent, and after pneumonia, bereavement, shingles, and various injuries over the years, I had come close, achieving silver medals at two world championships. I once read about an Australian para-rugby player who was so distraught at winning silver at a para-Olympics that he placed the silver medal on his bedside cabinet so that it was the first thing he saw when he woke up every morning to fire up his training each day. He won gold at the next games. I did the same thing with the silver medal from Pontevedra.

Lesson: never give up, dreams can come true.

Time

The pandemic put the quest for gold on hold as travel was either banned or highly restricted, and most triathlon events around the world were cancelled in 2020 and into 2021. I finally left financial services, this time for good, at the end of February 2021, deciding to retire from State Street a few months before the 3-year earn-out concluded in order to try to support my Dad in his grief. I was 52 years old and retired, which I'd worked hard for and looked forward to, but it was still a strange feeling. I was looking forward to having more time and not having to rush to squeeze training into early mornings or evenings, but I was also aware I probably needed to keep busy in other ways.

When I first met Matt Bottrill in early 2019, he was aware that one day I had plans to do some triathlon coaching, and he'd said to me that when I retire, I should get back in touch to see if there were any opportunities with his coaching company. In March 2021, I dropped him a line, and in April, I started working part-time as a self-employed coach with Matt Bottrill Performance Coaching, MBPC.

Around the same sort of time, I also took the decision to become self-coached again, so I parted ways with Bill and Simon, partly to reduce monthly outgoings given I had no regular income anymore and partly as I wanted flexibility in my program given the extra time I would now be able to exploit.

For example, if it happened to be a sunny Monday and I had no other plans, I was keen to simply head off and ride my bike for a few hours. I'll always be grateful to Simon and Bill for all of their help and advice over the years. Indeed, we'd given Bill the nickname 'Wol'[19] given his penchant for delivering pearls of wisdom at critical junctures in the training process.

Racing did return in 2021, but we made the decision to remain in the UK, given the complexities of international travel during the second year of the pandemic. There were more lockdowns and various restrictions imposed and removed during the year, which made planning difficult, and we also wanted to be cautious, given we were members of support bubbles for both of our elderly Dads. I entered a local middle distance race, the Cotswold 113, to kick the season off in June, with the main A race being the British Middle Distance National Champs, to be held in Aberfeldy in Scotland in August.

I did enjoy the freedom with regard to training; it was just the luxury of not having to rush, which was so liberating. I didn't ramp up training volume significantly, conscious of doing my ageing body some mischief, averaging almost 16 hours per week in 2021, compared to just over 15 hours in 2020.

The main changes in training were the introduction of regular flexibility and mobility work, consistent strength training, more swim volume (when pools were open) and an increase in time on the bike. The house we had bought in Cheltenham was conveniently located for a pool, which was situated at the end of the road and only a 5-minute walk away. I had no excuses not to swim regularly and started to get into a habit of swimming most weekday mornings, with sessions usually lasting an hour. It was a

---

[19] For those that don't know their Winnie The Pooh, this is the name of the owl character in the books

significant change from dashing to a pool during my lunch break to squeeze in a 30-minute session.

Sadly and mysteriously, the increased swim frequency and volume does not seem to have resulted in any noticeable improvements in my swim performance! However, I am a firm believer that the impact of the swim on the rest of the triathlon race is either ignored or under-rated by many, and I do think the extra volume has made me more efficient and, therefore, fresher for the bike and run, even though the absolute swim times haven't fallen.

I think the other major effects of semi-retirement were the decrease in overall stress and the availability of time to better space out sessions and focus on recovery. I was able to fuel more easily after every session and schedule regular massages and daily maintenance, such as foam rolling. The lack of travel due to work was particularly enjoyable as the novelty of business travel had worn off about 20 years ago. No more landing in Sydney at 6 am, after a 22-hour journey, dashing to the hotel to get changed and squeeze a short run in before a day of meetings. I was lucky to be in this position at the tender age of 52 and keen to fully make the most of it.

The Cotswold 113 race in June came around quickly, and it felt good to be racing again after so long. I hadn't raced since Oman in February 2020, and I expected to feel a bit rusty, so the plan for the race was simply to have fun and blow the cobwebs away. I managed just to win the 50-54 age group, overtaking Dave Mantle on the run and managing to hold him off to win by just over a minute.

The same race organiser held a similar event at the same location in early July, the Cotswold Classic, so I entered that for the next race. Covid restrictions had been lifted to such an extent that Matt, Katie, Jack, and Vic all stayed with us for the weekend as they were also racing (apart from Vic). Our friend Alex, who lived locally, was also on the start list, and it felt good to be getting back to racing with friends.

As often seems to be the case with this race, the venue was shrouded with fog when we arrived for the early start and showed little sign of shifting, resulting in a delayed start. Time ticked by, and the stubborn fog sat over the lake, finally forcing the organisers to cancel the swim and turn the race into a bike and run only as they needed to ensure they could still adhere to the agreed times to reopen roads. It wasn't ideal, and the start ended up as a bunfight as people rushed to transition to shed their wetsuits and grab their bikes. I headed off a little discombobulated, which was going to increase further as I witnessed some of the most blatant drafting I've seen in a race, including by guys I knew in my age group.

At one point, I was catching a group of four guys, who I could see were working in a very structured 'through and off' fashion, with each rider taking short turns on the front. Incensed, I burnt a box of matches to go by them, only for them to catch me later down the road and pour salt into the wound as the guy on the back said I should jump his wheel as they went by. I politely declined, adding they were a bunch of cheating tossers. Another race where the run was largely fuelled by annoyance, but it worked, and I won my age group by just over 3 minutes. Alex won the race overall, and Jack came 3rd overall, so it was a successful, albeit foggy, morning in the end.

The day got considerably worse, however. We returned home later that day, and Luce got a call from one of her Dad's carers. She had visited his house as planned only to find the newspaper still sticking out of the letterbox and unable to get an answer to the doorbell. We headed over at speed to find him collapsed outside in the garden where he had fallen the previous evening. He was conscious but in obvious distress and following the call for an ambulance he was admitted to Gloucester Royal Hospital that evening. Hospital visiting was still very restricted due to the pandemic, so nobody was allowed into A&E with him.

Lucy, her sister and partner, Caxster and BH, and I waited outside, peering through the window of a closed door, a memory that still haunts me. Luce managed to find a kind member of staff who let her and Caxster in briefly but found that their Dad had pretty much been abandoned on a trolley without even a drink of water, which given he was incredibly dehydrated from lying outside for several hours, was just awful care.

I won't go into all of the details of the ensuing 8 days, as this is not the place, but it was a very stressful and upsetting period, with Paddy receiving a standard of care which was frankly shocking. He was discharged and readmitted a couple of times, from both Gloucester and Cheltenham, until the following weekend when he collapsed again in his bedroom. Luckily, Luce's oldest sister, Jo, was staying with him that evening, and an ambulance was called again.

This time, the staff at Gloucester finally diagnosed heart failure, and Luce sat down with Paddy and the consultant on Monday to discuss the required procedure to replace the problematic heart valve. That evening, Paddy very sadly died in hospital. Although we now had experience of parental bereavement, the shock and heartbreak were just as traumatic.

I was close with Paddy. We shared many similar interests, such as a love of cricket, rugby, birdy num nums, and truthful journalism, an interest in current affairs, history, and science, and similar values in a desire for justice and fairness. His loss left a huge hole in the lives of many people, obviously his family, but many others, including myself. In less than 4 years, three of our four parents had died in what felt like quick succession, and the grief compounded accordingly. We miss them all terribly, talk about them a lot, and thankfully, now largely share happy memories and anecdotes.

In terms of racing, I returned to Cowman to help prepare for Aberfeldy later in August, but my heart really wasn't in it. It went ok, an age group win and 9th overall, but it was one of those rare occasions where I found little joy in racing. The grief we were experiencing whilst still trying to care for my lonely and distraught Dad was weighing very heavily on our shoulders. We took the decision to carry on with the plan to go to Scotland for the weekend for the Aberfeldy race, with the hope that a brief change of scene may help, as it did a little in 2018 when we went to Cascais. Unfortunately, a wet Aberfeldy bears little resemblance to a warm, sunny Cascais, but it was good to get away.

The weather on race day morning was awful, with the forecasted heavy rain starting prior to the start and persisting until almost the end of the bike leg. I had a surprisingly good swim, coming out of the water in the lofty heights of second place in the age group. The loch was pretty chilly, so I layered up in transition, conscious that

I wanted to avoid getting cold on the bike. I headed off in the rain on what would be a beautiful bike course on a bright, sunny morning.

The bike headed up from the start, which was good in terms of trying to get warm, but meant there was a pretty technical descent towards the end of the course. Once I'd warmed up, I felt good on the bike and put down the fastest split in the age group on a course that didn't naturally suit me and in tough conditions, so I was very pleased to head out onto the run in first place.

By now, the rain had stopped, the sun had started to come out, and I once again had the thought, 'At least I'm now going to at least finish.' A 1:28 run split was also the fastest in the age group, and I won the 50-54 middle-distance national title again by almost 6 minutes. A good day was put very quickly into perspective, however, when the news started to come out that another of the athletes, Nathan Ford, had crashed on the bike and was in a very serious condition in hospital with a broken neck. Nathan survived but his life is forever changed, both physically and mentally. His story shocked the triathlon community, which quickly rallied to help and raise money for his care.

After spending a few lovely days in the Lake District on the way home, I got back to work, briefly, to prepare for the last race of the season, the inaugural Outlaw[20] middle-distance race at Bowood House in Wiltshire. Aberfeldy had filled me with confidence after another challenging year, and I was looking forward to racing an

---

[20] Outlaw are probably the largest triathlon race organiser in the UK and their races are the only ones that really compete with Ironman in terms of professionalism and organisation

Outlaw race for the first time. I was also enjoying the coaching, with the number of athletes increasing to 8-10 over the year, which was about the right number I was finding. I wanted to ensure I gave each athlete sufficient time and was, therefore, keen to keep the number relatively small. I was also finding that designing and reviewing training programs, providing feedback, researching new developments and trying to deliver the best service I could was more time-consuming than I had anticipated.

In terms of training program design, I had reached the general conclusion over the years that the really fine details of individual sessions, e.g. should the duration of a specific interval be 60 or 90 seconds, were secondary to ensuring the overall structure and balance is appropriate for an athlete.

Ensuring the program is achievable whilst providing the progressive load to elicit adaptation can only be done on an individual basis, as everyone has different life constraints, strengths, weaknesses, training environments, etc. How coaches manage to look after, say, 20-30 athletes, I have no idea!

In terms of my own program, I do have a handful of 'favourite' sessions that I have used as benchmarks to assess where I am over the years. For the swim, the classic 'Red Mist,' as named by the swim coaching company SwimSmooth, falls into this category, comprised of 10 x 400, with 25-40 seconds rest intervals depending on fitness, where the objective is to increase the pace of the 400's throughout the session, with the last one as the fastest of the lot. This is not straightforward to achieve, and on many occasions, I've blown up on the 8th or 9th repetition.

On the bike, it is the VO2 max set constructed from 10 x 3 minutes at approximately 110-120% of FTP, depending on fitness, with 3 minutes of easy spinning in between. Again, the goal is to try to build the intervals, both within the 3 minutes and across the session, with the highest 3-minute power for the last interval. This session hurts, and you need to be in the right headspace beforehand to give yourself the best chance of nailing it.

Sticking with the theme of ten, on the run, I'll often fall back on the simple 10 x 1km at threshold pace, with 60-second easy jog recoveries in between. I like to execute this session on a treadmill to remove the disruption of crossing roads or gradients, and the objective is to build the pace throughout the session, with the last couple of intervals above threshold if fitness allows.

Outlaw Half Bowood was a good way to finish off the season as, for what felt like the first time that year, the weather on race day was lovely. I was impressed with Outlaw as a race organiser, and the event was fantastic, with a lovely atmosphere, held in the grounds of Bowood House. A decent swim, only about 90 seconds off the leader, set me up and I set off on my bike in the September sunshine feeling good. The course was great, rolling and fast, and I thoroughly enjoyed not battling my way through any driving rain and wind.

I came into transition in the lead and commenced the 3-lap hilly run course around the grounds of the stately home. I held onto the lead, and winning the age group meant I'd remained undefeated in the 50-54 category over the 2021 season, something that I don't think I'd achieved before, probably because there had been no major championships to race at!

As 2021 ended, it started to become clear that the worst of the pandemic was over, and it was looking increasingly likely that 2022 was going to resemble a more normal year. International travel was going to be possible, and a full calendar of race events was scheduled, so unless a new variant threw a complete spanner in the works, we assumed we could plan for a more normal year.

The thought of international travel was a little daunting, which sounds bizarre, I know, especially as pre-pandemic, we were such seasoned travellers. At the time, it felt like the period 2020-21 was going to change everything, but how wrong we were; it is quite incredible how quickly 'normality' returned, although some of the positives of that period didn't endure, sadly. For a brief period, there appeared to be an increased sense of community in the UK, and not just exemplified by the Thursday evening 'clap for carers,' but by a greater collective sense of care. Remarkable really given the woeful leadership the people of the UK had to suffer, it certainly wasn't leadership by example.

However, we quickly returned to the polarised world of individualism, fuelled by keyboard warriors on social media, who ensure that every debate and topic is denigrated into conflict. Sad. I also miss the really quiet roads during lockdown. They were definitely the days that I most enjoyed riding my bike in the UK.

We decided to kick off 2022 with a return trip to Majorca in May for the Ironman 70.3 race, where I still had unfinished business following punctures and hypothermia in 2014 and 2016, respectively. Even though it was only a short-haul trip for a week to somewhere very familiar, we still found packing difficult, having got completely out of the habit of going anywhere! However, once there, we quickly settled into the rhythm of remembering what a holiday felt like and had a lovely week in the sunshine.

Frustratingly, I had another disappointing race, coming 8th in my age group and absolutely miles behind the winner, Paul Lunn. Paul is a legend in the triathlon world and we overlap in the age group, thankfully, for only the last year before I go up again. I haven't, and won't ever, come close to beating him, so I just have to accept that racing at the top end of the age group is always a challenge.

I wasn't, therefore, frustrated to lose to Lunny, that is a given, it was more how I felt. I couldn't put my finger on it, but I just felt a bit flat, and blood tests later would confirm that I did have some thyroid issues around this time, which may have been a contributing factor. The GP didn't put me on any medication as he was hopeful that the thyroid would correct naturally as the hormone imbalance wasn't significant, which it thankfully did after a few weeks.

Next up was a return to the local Cotswold 113 middle-distance race in early June, and a feeling of déjà vu descended as we drove down to the venue that morning, watching dark clouds mass on the horizon. Another wet and cold experience produced another disappointing performance and result, with plenty of shivering on the bike, even with arm warmers and an additional layer, contributing to a 2nd place in the age group.

My confidence was low and I really needed a boost before heading to Samorin in Slovakia towards the end of August for the Long Distance World Championships. I was hoping that the inaugural Ironman 70.3 at Swansea in early August would provide that. Before then, we had another trip to the Alps planned for some riding, hanging out with mates and watching the Tour de France in July. It was a wonderful holiday, starting in Megève, where Luce, although now testing negative, was still recovering from Covid.

We've found that when either of us has caught Covid, it has resulted in elevated heart rates when exercising for some time afterwards, and this time was no exception, so some caution was required. We then relocated for a week to Bourg d'Oisans, where we rented a large house and were joined by Matt, Katie, Jack, Vic, Dan, Kate and Kris. It was a great week, lots of good riding, plenty of laughs and the creation of many special memories.

Remarkably, the weekend we spent in Swansea was blessed with warm sunshine and light winds, an outcome we were not expecting. I was grateful for the dry roads as the bike course was very technical around the Gower peninsula, and wet, sketchy roads would have made it even trickier. We had another lovely weekend with friends as Jack and Alex were both racing, so we spent time with them and Vic, Jess and Jack's parents, Mel and Paul.

The race provided the confidence boost I was looking for, kicking off with a decent swim in the jellyfish-infested dock, heading out on my bike in 5th place in the age group. For the first time this year, I felt good on the bike and seemed to handle a course unsuited to me reasonably well, avoiding the livestock on the roads and generally having a good time. I was chuffed with the 2:41 bike split, the 3rd fastest in the age group, and headed out of transition in third, just behind the guy in second. I quickly passed him and settled into a lovely 2-lap run around the bay.

Prior to the race, Luce and I had discussed that the objective was simply to secure a 70.3 world championship slot for the following year, so I just had to cruise the rest of the course and hold on to second. I was aware of the guy in the lead and saw at the far turnaround on the first lap that I was closing on him fast, confirmed by Luce as I headed back towards town when she excitedly pointed out that the leader was only just in front of me. I smiled and reeled him in, taking the lead at the end of the first lap and holding on to it for the win with a 1:28 run split, the fastest in the category. I was very happy, both with the result but more importantly the performance; I'd felt good racing and was feeling more confident about the worlds in a couple of weeks time.

We flew to Vienna on Wednesday, 17th August, before getting a transfer across the border to Samorin in Slovakia. The world champs were being held at the X-bionic sphere, an Olympic training venue on the banks of the Danube, not far from Bratislava. The disruption from the pandemic had obviously resulted in difficulties for governing bodies to organise events and find venues that were happy to host them. World Triathlon decided to partner with a recently created organisation, the Professional Triathletes Organisation, PTO, which was already hosting the triathlon equivalent of golf's Ryder Cup, the Collins Cup, at X-bionic.

This relatively last-minute plan did mean that the race was a different format, reverting to the distance used by the PTO, which was a 2km swim, 80km bike and 18km run to make up their T100 distance, instead of the usual 3km, 120km and 30km for the normal long distance world championships. I wasn't too phased and was just looking forward to competing again, even though I was in the last year of the age group, and my old nemesis, Olaf, was on the start list.

The out-and-back bike course was pancake flat, so I'd taken the time to arrange to put a bigger chain ring on my bike prior to flying out, and I was glad I did. As race day approached, it was clear that the wind was going to play a major role, with the outbound bike leg likely to have a massive tailwind, but the return leg would be a suffer-fest into a very strong headwind on exposed roads.

Luce and I sat in the hotel room and discussed a strategy, agreeing that my only real chance relied on me taking Olaf as early as possible on the bike to create a larger buffer on the run than I had had in Romania in 2019 and then just hold on for dear life. It sounded like a marvellous plan to me, and I was ready to give it full gas. As my Swiss friend Marcel had once told me, 'You are so strong on zee bike,' and I knew I'd have to squeeze out every ounce of that strength on Sunday.

Thankfully, the race officials didn't ban disc wheels on race day morning, even though it was blowing an absolute hoolie, and I set up in transition in a surprisingly calm state. The Danube is a big river, I mean, absolutely bloody massive, and that morning, it looked like an angry ocean with some large waves whipped up by the high winds. It was a tough swim but I had got used to tricky conditions over the years and just tried to stay calm and focus on one stroke at a time.

I exited the water in 2nd place in 50-54 but had given up just over 4 minutes to Olaf, even though it was wetsuit legal, so I knew I had a lot of work to do. I got my head down and disappeared down the road like a nutter, thoroughly enjoying the tailwind and searching for Olaf's German tri-suit. By the time I reached the turnaround at 40km, in 53 minutes, averaging just over 28mph, I still hadn't seen Olaf and was starting to worry that I was staring down the barrel of the score going to 7-0.

The return leg was brutal. I tried to stay aero and ground my way back down the road, thinking that if I'm struggling, and I tend to be a relatively strong rider into the wind, then everyone else must be suffering. Just before the 60km mark, I spotted the German colours ahead of me, and as I closed on him, I could confirm it was Olaf. I went by, obviously trying to appear that I was cruising along on a Sunday jolly when I was probably pushing around 320-330 watts, and thought, 'Ok, the race starts now, I need to gap him as much as possible.'

With only 20km to go, I knew it was a big ask to build a significant lead, but I mullered myself like I hadn't ever done so before. I came into transition with Graham Baxter, who was now in the age group above me and someone I would not have expected to catch on the bike, so I knew I had ridden well. The fastest T2 in the age group saw me heading out onto the run with a lead of over 4 minutes, so the objective of building a bigger lead than Romania had been achieved, but I obviously wasn't confident it was necessarily enough.

The 3-lap run course looped around the sports venue, including an out-and-back section on an elevated stretch of the banks of the Danube. My legs felt good, and I was relieved to hear from Luce that the gap was staying pretty constant during the first lap. On the second lap, I could tell that the gap had even grown a little when I got eyes on Olaf coming back down the stretch on the river bank. I think it was at this point that I started to believe.

By the third lap, I was starting to struggle to keep my emotions in check and just focus on trying to maintain cadence, form and not think too far ahead. As I entered the finish chute, grabbing the Union flag from Luce, my emotions came flooding out, crossing the line in a bit of a state of disbelief that I had actually achieved this ridiculous goal of becoming an age group world champion.

Mum, you were right, and I thought of her, Kate and Paddy as I crossed the line. We celebrated that evening with Clive Granger, an athlete I was coaching at the time who had won bronze in the 55-59 category, and his wife, drinking a lot of gin in the hotel bar and hanging out with some of the professionals who had raced in the Collins Cup over the weekend.

Yes, I'm aware that if there are any haters reading this, they'd be saying to themselves it was a poxy championship, with a shortened and weak start list at an event that nobody really cares about; it wasn't Kona for God's sake, at a time coming out of the pandemic when people still weren't travelling much. And anyway, who cares about age group titles, especially for old gits in their mid-fifties. But I didn't, and still don't, care. I'd set myself an objective, a dream really, and after many years, I had finally accomplished it.

I can't say I've been dreaming about it since 2004, when I started triathlon. If you'd asked me about world championships back then, I would have thought you were completely mad, but as you will have read if you've got this far, over the years, the goalposts have gradually and incrementally moved, evolving to become a dream that I really wasn't sure was remotely realistic. I was ecstatic, and just as importantly, I finally had a score on the board. Olaf 6, Pete 1.

Looking back, I think having the luxury of time once I'd retired in

February 2021 played a big part in finally achieving this goal. Again, not necessarily because of significantly increased volume, although I was starting to get signs that I was a 'volume responder' when it came to the bike, but because of the luxury of scheduling sessions better, having more time to recover and fuel better, no work stress and getting more sleep.

The alarm wasn't blaring at 5 am every morning, and I had been consistently getting 7-8 hours of sleep per night for probably the first time in my life. I knew how lucky I was to have the luxury of this time, but I had consciously chosen to take the retirement option and not pursue more material wealth. Time is such a valuable luxury that, paradoxically, you only really start to realise as you get older.

I could finally put the silver medal on my bedside cabinet away.

Lesson: time is the most valuable commodity and worth every penny.

Finally

Coming back down from the high of Samorin took a little while, and certainly longer than the 24 hours that Magness and Stulberg recommend you should spend celebrating successes. It had been such a long road, with twists and turns along the way, that I felt it was important to take some time to reflect. The 2022 season wasn't over though, with the European Middle Distance Championships in Bilbao towards the end of September and the Ironman 70.3 World Championships[21] in St George, Utah, towards the end of October.

With the main outcome goal now achieved in Samorin, I did have people ask me if I was now going to retire from triathlon and what would motivate me to continue. I had no plans to retire, mainly because I simply loved training and racing, regardless of any race outcome. Many people say that triathlon, and sport in general, is not just a hobby but forms a lifestyle, and it has certainly evolved that way for me.

Also, although outcome goals such as winning races and medals obviously mattered to me, I was also very focused on the process. I think it was again Brad Stulberg who said that you shouldn't focus on being the best but the best at getting better, and this resonates with me. I am always looking at ways to improve my 'craft,' either through refining training methods, technique tweaks, race strategy, equipment improvements, better habits around nutrition and recovery, etc. It is one of the attractions of triathlon

---

[21] The originally planned 2020 championships for Taupo, New Zealand had been pushed back and were going to end up getting held in December 2024.

in that there are always ways to be looking to improve, even for someone in their sixth decade.

In addition, I have always largely been intrinsically motivated. I don't have much of a social media presence, with no Facebook account, not many followers on a private Strava account and limited Instagram activity. I only started posting on the latter once I started coaching with Matt Bottrill as I thought it may, in a very small way, help his business.

Otherwise, I would avoid it like the plague. My Strava account isn't private because I worry about my rivals seeing my training. I couldn't care less about that, as there are no secret "magic bullet" sessions. It is purely because such extrinsic 'rewards' in the form of kudos and likes from people I don't know really don't get my motivational juices flowing. Of course, I'm not so naïve that I don't get some buzz from extrinsic recognition, but only from those people around me whose opinions I value and who matter to me.

Back to Bilbao, another city that we hadn't visited that triathlon was taking us to, this time with Lucy's oldest school friend, Christine. It was a good trip, and we enjoyed exploring Bilbao on the warm, sunny days leading up to the race. Race day, however, was not blessed with such weather, and the heavens opened once again, which made the relatively technical bike course interesting.

For reasons that nobody understood, it was an afternoon start, but at least unlike Ibiza in 2018, this was known upfront, and pre-race fuelling could be planned accordingly. The swim in the river that bisects the city went well until the exit, which required hauling yourself onto a high pontoon. There are photos of me scrambling onto this pontoon, looking very much like a large beached walrus, but finally, I managed to exit and jumped on my bike for a soggy ride. I had a good ride and thankfully didn't suffer from the cold on the descents in the rain, coming into T2 in the bronze medal position.

A 1:29 run, however, wasn't enough to stay on the podium, with another very fast German chap running a 1:21, pushing me back into 4th. I was Charles, but I wasn't disappointed, I felt like I'd had a good race across swim, bike, and run, and there was nothing else I could have done to change my performance. Sometimes, you just have to accept there are faster guys on the start line that day. Coming 4th was tempered by the fact that one of the athletes I was coaching, Mel Hayes, got bronze in the 55-59 age group, and I was chuffed to bits for her.

Preparing for St George was now the focus, although it was a little derailed as I'd picked up a bit of a niggle in my right knee, which seemed to be affecting my ability to put power down on the bike. I managed it over the next few weeks with a view to getting it sorted in the off-season once we were back from the US[22]. We were excited about the trip as our good friends from Canada, Dean and Soph, were flying down from Montreal to spend a week with us in Utah. We first met them in 1991 when I spent the summer at Ottawa University doing some research in the Chemistry department to decide whether to start a PhD or not, and we became firm friends very quickly. Alex and Jess were also travelling, together with another local triathlete who Alex was friends with,

____

[22] Which I did via Dan Wilkinson at Origin Health, who used shockwave to sort out the tendon above the kneecap, a treatment I hadn't experienced before and I was very impressed!

Stephen Derrett, who also swam at the pool I used. After the race, we had planned a few days at a resort in the Utah desert to unwind and relax properly. The holiday was fantastic, with one particular highlight being the day we all drove over to Bryce Canyon, which is absolutely stunning.

I was relaxed about the race. The start list was bonkers, and I knew I had my work cut out to come anywhere decent, even if I'd been uninjured, with folks like Lunny racing. So the plan was to enjoy it and see it as a celebration, which was lucky really, as I only managed to come 33rd! Race day morning was cold, I think only about 3-5 degrees, so we'd made a Walmart trip beforehand to stock up on warm gear, including hand and feet warmers and foil blankets. I put the foot warmers in my bike shoes and cut off some of the foil blankets to stuff down my trisuit, thinking I was as prepared as I could be, but the first 60 mins on the bike were still very cold. I'd had a terrible swim and tried to push hard on the bike but knew I wasn't riding as well as I could, and the 32nd fastest split in the age group, on terrain that should have suited me, confirmed this.

The run was hilly, and I gave it everything I had, celebrating the fact that we were in what is an iconic triathlon location with friends and having a good time. However, upon finishing, I did sit there thinking how much I was looking forward to going up to the 55-59 category the following year and leaving all these rapid 50-year-old youngsters behind, for a while at least.

I had increased my training volume in 2022, averaging just under 17 hours per week, and the plan for 2023 was to gradually increase further, largely through more swim and bike volume. The first race of the season was the World Triathlon Long Course World Champs in early May in Ibiza, and I was motivated to try and defend my title.

With this A race occurring early in the season, Luce and I discussed changing things to help try to get some decent bike volume done outside on the road beforehand, which can be tricky in the UK. We decided that I should try a training camp for the first time, focusing on the bike, with Stuart Hall Cycling in Majorca at the end of March. It was a good experience, and it confirmed what I suspected: that my bike fitness seems to respond well to higher volumes.

Two of the guides were semi-professional riders, and it was very helpful trying to sit on their wheels and just observe how they rode, when they changed gear, when they got out of the saddle, how they accelerated out of corners, etc. There weren't many triathletes on the camp, so I did get a fair bit of grief for not conforming with the 'roadie' rules, some of which seemed a tad obscure and, dare I say it, petty. For example, I wasn't ever sure why wearing a Garmin watch was a problem or why socks had to come up to mid-calf, but I smiled and shrugged, replying with the explanation that it was obviously because I was a triathlete.

Having the time to go out and just focus on training was fantastic, and I managed to clock up 55 hours of training over a 2-week period that included the camp. I headed home with increased confidence and finished off the Ibiza build over the rest of April. Ibiza was another trip and event that we shared with friends and family, including Jack, Vic, Jack's parents, Mel and Paul, Alex, Jess, Alex's grandparents, Bill and Lynn, and Caxster. We had a great laugh and thoroughly enjoyed the time leading up to the race, which didn't suffer this year with thunderstorms as we had experienced in 2018. It was still relatively tricky to sight on the swim due to the size of the swell, and I'm sure I swam a lot more than 3km, but I ran up the beach in 5th place. I had a blast on the 2 lap bike course, delivering the fastest split in 55-59 and entering T2 in second place, but just behind the Canadian guy who was leading. The Majorca bike volume seemed to have paid off, and I quickly ran down the Canuck as we headed out of transition to take the lead.

The run course was interesting, 3 and a half laps, including some technical sections around Ibiza's old town with cobbles and steep gradients. By the end of the first lap, Luce happily let me know that I had a decent lead, I can't remember how many minutes, but it was enough for me to think that the win was a possibility. This all changed on the second lap when I was informed of a very fast-running Italian guy, who I'd never raced before and was rapidly eating into my lead. I managed to just hold him off on the 3rd lap, but he ran up alongside me as we exited the transition area for the last time for the last half a lap or so to the finish.

Unlike in Romania, there was no running shoulder to shoulder; he just eased down the road, and I could do nothing but just watch him gradually disappear and, with him, the gold medal. I ended up finishing 55 seconds behind him, a pretty small margin in a race that had lasted almost six and a half hours, and I was gutted.

Watching him in tears with his family in the finish area was heart-warming and helped ease my disappointment, although I wasn't quite ready for the very passionate and sweaty Italian hug from both him and then his Dad. First loser again, for the third time at this event.

Next up was the Ironman 70.3 race in Luxembourg, a first outing for my new bike, the latest Trek Speed Concept. The race was 'just for fun' as I'd already got a slot for this year's world champs by winning at Swansea the previous year.

Another of Lucy's school friends, Jacquie, aka The Jaxster, was joining us in Luxembourg with her boyfriend, Glenn, to take on her first 70.3 race. It was a very hot weekend, and I couldn't believe it when they announced on race day morning that the swim in the Moselle River was going to be wetsuit-legal. They must have thrown some ice in just before dipping the thermometer as it was absolutely sweltering, even at 7 am. I didn't complain, happily squeezing my sweaty limbs into my wetsuit and setting off for a decent swim; I exited in just over 29 minutes in 5th place. The bike was fantastic fun, and I loved the new bike, which I'd stuck another larger chain ring on and hammered around the European countryside in the warm sunshine.

Fortunately, my lead as I exited T2 was large enough to have a very cautious run as the heat was now oppressive, so I walked aid stations, took on fluids, and deposited ice up and down every orifice. It was a lovely event, made even more special by clapping Jaxster over the line to complete her first Ironman 70.3, a mighty impressive feat given the conditions.

The season continued with the British Middle Distance National Champs, this year to be hosted by Outlaw at their race at the Holkham estate in Norfolk. Our mate Jack was now doing the official media photography for Outlaw, so he and his Dad, Paul, stayed with us for the weekend at an Airbnb in nearby Wells on the coast.

Alex, who I had started coaching earlier in the year, was also racing. It was another great weekend, a lovely vibe at the race venue, definitely helped by a dose of good weather. I was chuffed with the performance, 2nd out of the water and then the fastest bike and run splits in the age group to take the 55-59 national title. I'd got my bike's front end adapted by Matt Bottrill, and it felt fantastic, very comfortable, and just 'right,' which contributed to the bike performance on a fast course where most of the time was spent on the poles.

The run was lumpy, and I was aware my lead wasn't huge, so I was running scared, always listening out for someone catching me. However, I hung on and enjoyed the finish chute. It was a good day, with Alex winning his age group and coming 3rd overall in another very rapid sub 4 hours time. I was so pleased for him, fulfilling his enormous potential.

Next up was a return to the quest of getting on the podium at the Ironman 70.3 World Championships and a trip to Lahti in Finland in August, another location we had never heard of, never mind thought of visiting. Training had gone well, and the Luxembourg and Holkham performances had injected some confidence, something that I've found to be just as important as the physical side.

Getting the balance right between not getting too cocky and complacent but also having some confidence in your form was something I'd struggled with over the years, as I generally always erred on the side of lacking a bit of confidence. Whilst tapering in the week before the race, I headed off for a run on the day before we were due to fly and had to abort as I had a sudden onset of pain in the right lower calf/soleus, and very quickly, a lump swelled up. I'd never experienced anything like it before and wasn't sure what it might mean for race day. I sent the photos to Dan at Focus Soft Tissue, who had been helping Luce and I for a few years with regular massage treatment, but we were none the wiser. I tried not to worry, and we flew off to Helsinki as planned.

Lahti was a strange sort of place; parts of it certainly seemed to give away that it wasn't all that long ago that it was effectively part of the Soviet empire. The countryside around the city was lovely, very wooded and rolling, which Alex and I experienced when we did a recce of the bike course on the Thursday before the race.

Unfortunately, race day weather once again disappointed. Checking the forecast that morning, it was due to be dry, but as I exited the swim and ran out of transition with my bike, a light rain started, which got steadily heavier. I got very cold, even though I was pushing hard in a big gear, and the last 40 minutes of the ride were spent shivering and frustrated at not being able to put down the power I knew I could. It was still a better bike performance than in St George the previous year, coming into T2 with the 8th fastest in the age group in 2:18, but I knew it should have been quicker.

The 2-lap run kicked off with a fairly long incline before descending back down to run alongside the lake and back to transition and the finish area. I felt good, and after a quick loo stop shortly after leaving transition, I focused on getting into a rhythm and ticking off the kilometres.

Bizarrely, my calf felt absolutely fine, even though the big lump was still there, so I just ignored it and cracked on. Luce told me I was in 5th, which for the Ironman events would get me on the podium as for reasons I didn't understand, the podium was 5 deep at their championships, which gave me a boost for the second lap.

One of the guys racing in my age group was Laurent Jalabert, the ex-professional cyclist. Running along the lakefront for the last time, he ran up alongside me with what seemed to be a couple of his mates. We ran side by side for a while before I edged ahead with about 2km to go, only for him to then come back past me about a kilometre later. I tried to force my legs to stay with him but just couldn't, possibly due to the disadvantage of not being a professional athlete in my youth, or years of allegedly and unknowingly taking EPO, or maybe both. I ended up finishing 6th, just 30 seconds behind Jalabert, who took the last spot on the podium.

It was my best performance so far at the 70.3 worlds, coming 8th in Zell, 7th in South Africa, and now 6th in Finland (I've excluded the disappointing performances at Nice and St George from this list!), so I was happy to still be progressing, and I was pleased with the performance.

At this rate of progress, I should be on the top step in another 5 years. There were some 'what if' thoughts afterwards as it did feel a little like an opportunity missed, but on balance, it was a very positive experience. Alex had another fantastic race, again coming in under 4 hours and putting to bed his disappointment at his experience at St George last year, where a pre-race tumble on his bike pre-race resulted in rib damage.

The 2023 season was due to finish at the Ironman 70.3 Emilia-Romagna race in Cervia, Italy, in September. Dean and Soph from Canada had planned an Italian holiday around the race and were coming to stay in Cervia for a few days before the race, which we were looking forward to. The trip was a real hoot, including a pasta and tiramisu-making lesson and culminating in a memorable race day, one of the most fun I've experienced.

Luce had organised VIP access, and Dean made the most of the prosecco on offer whilst meeting the Mayor of Cervia and generally having a good time. I had a great swim; sub 29 minutes was very rare for me nowadays, and I exited in 2nd place, ready to drop some watt bombs on what was going to be a very rapid bike course. The bike didn't disappoint, heading back into transition in first place to be greeted by Luce, Soph, and Dean, who by now was well-oiled and waving his selfie stick like a loon.

The temperature had risen considerably as it had been an afternoon race start, and the run course was baking hot. As with Luxembourg, I made the decision to be conservative given the lead I had and the fact that the only objective of the race, other than having fun, was to secure a slot for next year's world champs in New Zealand. It was mission accomplished, winning the race with a decent margin and having a lot of fun in the process.

I reflected on the season with some pride, another silver medal at the long course world champs, my best 70.3 world champs performance, another national middle distance title, and wins at Luxembourg and Italy. I'd also really enjoyed every moment of it and shared all the events with friends, creating lots more memories along the way. As my mind turned towards 2024, I started to get an itch. I thought I'd never need to scratch.

For many years I'd had the piss taken out of me for not doing a full Ironman and that, indeed, I wouldn't be a 'proper' triathlete until I had. The truth is that I hadn't had any interest, partly because I was aware that an Ironman was all about nutrition and that you couldn't properly race it (unless you're elite) as you had to constantly be focused on correct pacing.

This didn't appeal, especially on the bike, as one of the things I loved about middle-distance racing was that I could pretty much go full gas on the bike and have a lot of fun doing so. However, over the course of 2023, I started to increasingly think that I'd like to give an Ironman a go, just to see what it was like, but mainly as I was keen to try something different and set myself a new challenge.

I wasn't bothered about setting the fastest time I possibly could, and therefore, choosing a notoriously fast Ironman event such as Copenhagen or Hamburg. The key was to have a great experience, and after some thought, I entered Ironman Austria, which was celebrating its 25th anniversary in 2024. The course looked stunning, and we had thoroughly enjoyed our previous Austrian trips to Kitzbuhel, Zell, and Walchsee, so I tentatively pressed the enter button. Even after all these years of competing at triathlon, including various long-distance events, the thought of a full Ironman still got the nervous juices flowing, which I decided was a good thing.

After spending a fantastic New Year in Lapland, attempting, but failing, to see the Northern Lights with our friends Matt and Alex, we flew back to the UK on January 1st to start the build towards

Austria, scheduled for June 16th. I frustratingly picked up an achilles niggle in February, but this time I spotted it early and acted decisively, getting three lots of shockwave treatment at Origin Health, which quickly sorted it out, and I was back running again towards the end of March. With the Ironman in mind, I decided to do another bike training camp in Majorca in March, this time with Andy Cook Cycling. My bike legs were feeling good, and I was looking forward to testing them at the inaugural Ironman Valencia 70.3 race in mid-April.

We travelled to Valencia with Alex, and the plan was to drive down the coast after the race for a week's riding in the Calp region. We had been toying with the idea of moving abroad and were going to check out this part of Spain as a potential location, although we quickly changed our minds when we realised it was largely populated with money launderers, gangsters, and Ronnie Biggs types. Valencia was fantastic and I managed another age group win, which, given my lack of run volume, I was very chuffed with. Alex also had a good race, clocking another sub 4 hours, making the overall podium and winning his category. We loved the city and the event and followed up a good weekend with some great riding around Calp.

Training for Austria resumed upon getting home, with the main difference to previous years being the increased duration of rides on my TT bike whilst practicing nutrition strategies. Given the gastrointestinal issues I'd had many years ago, I planned to stick to a non-solid nutrition strategy, using the SIS Beta product, both drinks and gels, to consume approximately 100 grammes of carbohydrates per hour. I knew that sticking to a power output that was largely at or below my first lactate threshold, or LT1, was key, and I tried to focus on achieving this during the long rides whilst training my gut to be happy with about 100g per hour of fuel. I only did a couple of century rides, and the longest run off the bike was an hour, but I was hoping that 20 years of endurance training would stand me in good stead come race day.

We flew into Ljubljana in Slovenia on the Wednesday before the race and drove over the border to Klagenfurt that evening. The venue was as beautiful as we had hoped for, with a crystal clear azure lake surrounded by mountains. The usual pre-race routine followed, scoping out the course and transitions, swimming in the lake, riding the bike course, and figuring out the run course. I was excited and nervous; the training had gone well, but I knew that lots of things could go wrong with an Ironman, given how long a day out it was with so many variables.

We stayed in the official hotel next to the swim exit and transition for simplicity, which was great, and met a lovely Swiss couple in the crowded dining room one evening. The guy was racing and had done many Ironman races over the years. I explained that this was my first and asked him for any tips, to which he responded that his top tip was not to have any coke on the run until after the 30km mark, after which the extra kick that the sugar and caffeine gives you will help get you home. I nodded and, as I'd heard it before, vowed to remember that one.

The weather looked changeable on race day, and the rain was coming down as I finished off setting up in transition that morning. It then stopped as we headed to the swim start with hundreds of other athletes and a palpable air of anxiety in the air. The dulcet tones of Paul Kaye on the PA system drifted over the swim start area as I started to prepare myself for what lay ahead. Paul is a legend at Ironman races, having commentated at many I'd done over the years.

A couple of days previously, Luce and I had heard him giving a talk to a group of athletes near transition, explaining that Austria had been his first Ironman and how important your why was when it came to getting to the finish line. His why was to make his kids from his recently estranged marriage proud, and he welled up as he spoke, setting both Luce and I off. I wasn't sure what my why was, certainly nothing as significant as Paul's, but I did want to do myself proud and prove to myself that I can still set ambitious goals at the ripe old age of 55.

The 3.8km swim was lovely, with no biff with the rolling start and beautifully clean water. The swim ended with a section leaving the lake and heading along a canal to the exit. This section seemed to go on for hours, so I was chuffed to exit in 10th place in the category in just over 62 minutes. The rain was still holding off and I jumped on my bike to enjoy the 180km 2-lap bike course. I loved the bike, it was tremendous fun, even when the rain started to hammer down on the second lap.

By the end of the first lap, I knew I was going well as Luce stood near transition waving a finger at me to indicate that I was already in the lead. I was riding sensibly, sticking to the planned power, and remembering to consume calories regularly. The finger was still being displayed as I tried to dismount without cramping every sinew in my hamstrings, finishing with a split of just over 5 hours and the fastest in the age group.

I had planned to run the marathon at approximately 3:20 – 3:30

pace as I felt surprisingly good heading out of T2, holding 3:20 pace comfortably for the first 15-20km. I knew that this would not last and that, at some point, the pain would kick in, but I was hoping that this point would be deferred until after the 30km mark. I was wrong.

Shortly after halfway, I just wanted to lie down under a bush, pathetically uttering to Luce that the wheels had come off on the side of the road. I knew I was being chased down and that my almost 5-minute lead exiting T2 was getting slowly eaten into. This is the point where the mental side is so important, and although I'd slowed down, I just had to keep going. I decided to totally ignore the advice and started downing cups of coke from the 23km mark, desperate to try anything to keep moving forward. The rain had returned, which was quite pleasant but not for spectators, and I do remember seeing Luce on her hire bike in the pouring rain, tearing along a road alongside the run course, screaming encouragement with a rain poncho billowing behind her like some sort of demented superhero. The depth of her support knows no bounds.

The lead continued to diminish, and I had, maybe not surprisingly, moved the goalposts from simply completing an Ironman to wanting to complete inside 10 hours to now desperately wanting to win my age group after leading for so long. With about 5km to go, I was overtaken by a guy who looked like he was in my age group, and for a second, my head went down, thinking the win had gone and this was just like Ibiza all over again.

However, given the rolling start at Ironman events, you never know if an individual started before or after you, so although it looked like he was now winning on the road, there was still a chance. I dug in, tried to summon all the grit I possessed, and kept him in sight until arriving at the finish area.

Luce told me it was important I remembered to ring the bell at the end of the finish chute, a tradition for first-timers, which I did, risking collapsing in cramp as the bell was positioned too high and required jumping off the ground to reach. I saw her by the finish, screaming like a banshee, but I couldn't quite make out the words. I crossed the line, assuming I'd come second. I hadn't. I'd won the 55-59 category by 52 seconds in 9 hours and 43 minutes and had managed to pick up the pace over the last 3km.

To say I was gobsmacked would be a huge understatement. When I entered approximately 9 months previously, I would never have thought I would win my age group at my first Ironman. I sat in the recovery tent, trying to eat pizza and kaiserschmarrn, an Austrian favourite of ours comprised of mashed-up pancakes and apples, trying to digest both the food and what had just happened. Luce handed my phone to another athlete heading into the tent, and I was emotional to see and read the volume of WhatsApp messages I'd received during the day.

Many friends and family at home had been tracking progress via the Ironman app and watching the lead gradually decrease throughout the run with bated breath. Steve summed it up well later, saying it was 'one of the great Ironman tracking experiences!' We made it back to the hotel, and after having a funny turn in the shower, where I just had to sit down for a while, we started to celebrate the day.

Later that evening, at dinner, the Swiss coke guy came over to congratulate me, calling me 'Mr. Understated.' I thanked him and also for his advice, which I'd totally ignored.

The following morning, we went to the awards ceremony and slot allocation for Kona. It was a privilege to receive the award from Paul Kaye, but we didn't hang around for the slot allocation. Going to Kona hasn't ever interested me, partly as the course just sounds a bit bleak and also because we didn't fancy it as a holiday destination, spending time surrounded by the ultimate Type A triathletes strutting around with their tops off. I know, each to their own, and I have huge admiration for anyone who qualifies and races on the Big Island; it is the peak of our sport. I'm also aware that folks can train and race for years on their quest for a Kona slot, and there was almost a little guilt at getting a slot at the first attempt and then declining to take it, but my Ironman career was already over. I had said one and done, and now that I'd had the perfect day that I don't think I'd be able to surpass, this reinforced the decision. I also quite liked the idea of remaining undefeated at the distance, but most importantly, I was finally a proper triathlete.

Lesson: getting older doesn't mean you shouldn't get out of your comfort zone

Gratitude

I have a lot to be very grateful for, and not just relating to triathlon. It has provided me with so much more than a healthy lifestyle; indeed, I've heard Luce say to people a few times, 'There are far worse things he could be obsessed with,' which is very true. The obsession started very early, immediately after finishing that first local sprint race in May 2004, and I have wondered over the years why that was. Not wanting to get too deep, but triathlon did arrive in my life when I was probably in need of something to focus on.

As briefly discussed all the way back in Chapter 1, Luce and I had been trying to start a family shortly after relocating to Amsterdam in 1998. After a few years, it became clear that this was going to happen naturally, so after much discussion, we decided that we would try IVF, and we'd want to do this back in the UK, hence the move back in late 2001.

After considerable research, we decided to use the ARGC clinic in London, which published the best success rates in the country for women of Lucy's age. If we were going to do this, we thought we'd give ourselves the best possible chance, whatever the financial cost, and we had to meet with the ARGC first for them to agree to take us on[23]. The quoted success rate per completed IVF cycle was around 33%, so the scientists in us decided up front that we would plan for 3 cycles. If there was still no success after the third cycle, we would end the process, no matter how difficult that decision

---

[23] In hindsight, one of the reasons for their impressive statistics was probably due to selection bias as I suspect they only accepted 'patients' with the greatest chance of success in terms of age, health etc

would be. We were both concerned about the long-term potential impact of the hormone treatment on Luce's health, and although we obviously desperately wanted children, we were not prepared to risk our health to do so, either physically or mentally. Deciding at the outset what our boundaries were, including that we would not pursue more advanced and less rigorously tested procedures, was the best decision we made.

These ramblings are about triathlon, so I'm not going to go into detail. However, suffice it to say, we were not successful in starting a family and decided to stop trying towards the end of 2002. We had discussed whether to pursue adoption but decided that it wasn't for us, partly because we had heard horror stories about how intrusive the vetting process was from social services at the time, resulting in some couples actually splitting up, and also because if we were to have children, I, selfishly, wanted them to be genetically ours. It was a dark and difficult time, and to some extent, we went through a grieving process for a family we weren't going to have.

Societal norms are that you grow up, get married, have kids, have grandkids, and grow old with your family around you. When I was growing up, I never imagined or indeed thought about the potential outcome that I wouldn't have kids; when you're young, you just assume it will happen one day. Not everyone around us was as supportive as we would have hoped for, including being told that we should stop wallowing at one point, but it took a very long time to come to terms with if we ever fully have.

When it dawns on you that you're not going to have a family, you start to question many things, including why you are working your nuts off, what your point in society, and what the hell you are going to do with your life. We booked a week's holiday in Cambodia to get away and to try to start the long healing process. Triathlon, therefore, came along when I was feeling quite aimless, lost, and with little purpose. It also provided something completely new to focus on. I clutched this new focus in 2004 with both hands, and the obsession began.

Other than providing a purpose during a difficult time in my life, triathlon has also provided me with the opportunity to travel, meet lots of like-minded people, and visit places we would never have gone to. For this I am very grateful. To date, I've had the good fortune to race on 4 continents in 24 different countries and create so many wonderful memories and experiences. There are too many highlights to mention, but 2024 proved to be a particularly memorable year for travel, with trips to Valencia, Austria, Australia, Marbella, and New Zealand.

After Austria, the focus switched to the Australian trip in August for yet another bash at the Long Course World Champs, to be held in Townsville in Queensland. The recovery from the Ironman took a good 3-4 weeks before I was back to proper training again, but the preparation for Townsville went well, and we were excited about the trip. The start list was relatively punchy and included the Aussie guy who had won my age group at the Ironman 70.3 World Champs in Finland the previous year, Mark Clough.

We flew out to Cairns via Singapore and landed a week before the race to try to get over the jet lag. This proved trickier than we anticipated, and we quickly realised that long-haul travel starts to get a whole lot more exhausting as you get older. We enjoyed a few days in Cairns before driving down to Townsville to prepare for the race. I had originally assumed that a swim in the Coral Sea in August would automatically be non-wetsuit, but this was not to be the case, which was great news, especially as Cloughie and others on the start list were great swimmers. Just had to worry about jellyfish, saltwater crocodiles, and sharks. The bike course was relatively technical, 3 laps around the town with a few faster sections, and the run was 2 laps up the coast and back.

As with Samorin, Luce and I discussed a strategy for the race and came up with a remarkably similar plan. Swim as hard as I can, given the constraints of my poor technique to minimise losses to Cloughie et al., bike like a madman to try to catch up to the pointy end of the race and then hang on for dear life on the run and see what that brings.

The plan worked out perfectly, although you wouldn't think so after giving up 7 minutes to Mark after the 3km swim. Getting onto the bike in 9th place, I knew I had a lot of work to do, so I got my head down. Thankfully, it was one of those days when the bike legs turned up, and I felt great from the off, quickly moving through the field and, importantly, feeling like I was riding the course well, braking late and accelerating aggressively out of the corners and turnarounds.

On the second lap, I saw Mark coming back down the road from one of the turnarounds, and I knew the gap was significantly less than 7 minutes, which provided me with some extra motivation to muller myself even more. I took the lead on the third lap, riding past Mark with less than 20km to go, and knew I needed to go full gas to build as big a lead as I could. The wind had now gotten up, which may have helped grow the lead as I entered T2 with about a 2-minute gap, more than I was expecting. I'd ridden 2:59 for the bike leg, which was a bit shorter than the advertised 120km, but the next nearest split in the age group was Mark at 3:08.

It was now hot, and the 30km run seemed very daunting on completely smashed legs from the bike, but the plan was working, so I exited transition in good spirits. Luce gave me splits, and by the end of the first lap, it was clear that my lead had extended significantly, and I could relax a little.

Again, I followed a conservative strategy by walking the aid stations and ensuring I was taking on fluids. There was a fair bit of Aussie sledging and banter on the course, 'Hey Pom, enjoying the Aussie weather, hot enough for yer?' etc., as I started to wilt during the later stages of the run. I tried to stay in the moment, thinking how lucky I was to have the time and resources to be racing on the other side of the world and the health and fitness to be competing at all, never mind in the lead.

Descending back into the finish area, the emotions started to flood out, and turning onto the blue carpet of the finish chute was a lovely moment. I stopped to give Luce a kiss, at which point the Aussie commentator started to surmise 'that he doesn't even know that lady,' grabbed the Union Jack, and crossed the line elated. Given it was the first world age group title, Samorin felt special, but this performance was just as important to me, especially as we were now fully out of the pandemic, the start list was deeper, and the race distances were now correct, unlike in 2022. We finished off what was a great trip with a few days on Bedarra island, where there was little to do other than completely relax and enjoyed a mid-season break.

Racing was due to resume towards the end of October, this time at the Ironman Marbella 70.3 race. The 2025 World Champs were going to be held in Marbella, so the plan was to try to get a slot whilst also getting a good look at the course. We planned a long weekend with Caxster and Claire, our 86-year-old friend who we had spent a lot more time with since her husband, David, died. It was Claire's first triathlon experience, and she seemed genuinely excited to come away with us and enjoy it.

Matt and Katie also travelled over as Matt had decided to race, and we once again spent a fun few days with family and friends in the land of money-launderers and gangsters. The race went well, but a mismeasured swim course resulted in very long swim times before a very challenging bike course with lots of climbing. I rode well and quickly moved through the field, taking the lead on the way back from the far turnaround before an incredibly rapid descent back into transition.

Starting the run, I had a 6-minute lead, which ordinarily would be enough to secure the win in my age group as not many guys in their late 50s are running 1:24-1:26, but today was not one of those days. A Spanish chap ran like a train, running a 1:20 and winning by about 6 minutes. It was the fastest run split I'd ever seen in the 55-59 age group, and it was a tad humbling, but it didn't detract from the enjoyment of the day, of which my over-riding memory is seeing Luce, Caxster, Claire and Katie in the stand next to the finish line, beers in hands and adorned with 'I love Marbella' straw Panama hats.

The final race of what was a very long season was the Ironman

70.3 world champs in Taupo, New Zealand, in mid-December. By the time I'd recovered from Marbella and started the final build in December, the mental fatigue of the year was starting to kick in. I love training, and it is part of a daily habit, but when trying to peak for races and pushing yourself to hit numbers in key sessions, it can become draining after many months. I did everything I thought I could without going over the edge and getting ill or injured, and we, together with Caxster and Luce's oldest school friend, Christine, set off for New Zealand in early December for a 3-week trip, which had originally been planned for 2020. The extra time difference and journey length compared to Cairns had an impact, and the jet lag, once again, took a long time to recover from. After a couple of days in Auckland, celebrating my 56th birthday and catching up with friends, we headed down to Taupo via Hobbiton.

Taupo was beautiful, and we had a fantastic time leading up to the race, enjoying the town and surroundings. The atmosphere was very special, possibly as such a large proportion of the town seemed so welcoming and excited for the event, with over 10% of the approximately 25,000 inhabitants volunteering to help out over race weekend. We were lucky with the weather, and race day was forecast to be dry, not too windy, and getting warm on the run.

It was a stacked field, and I knew I was going to have to have a good day in order to achieve my stretch goal of a Top 5 podium position. I felt good during the swim in the crystal clear lake, pushing hard, and was pleased with the 30-minute split, which was good for me in freshwater[24], but this only gave me 47th place in the

---

[24] I tend to go a little quicker in sea swims due to the extra buoyancy of the saltwater

age group. The bike leg started badly, dropping my chain for the first time ever as I tried to mount at the exit to transition, compounding the problem as the chain got stuck in the cassette. A kind volunteer helped by lifting up my bike wheel as I managed to get it free, and after what seemed like ages, I finally rode off up the road, angry and frustrated.

I might plan to drop my chain in every race as I think I had the best bike performance I've ever had. I felt good from the start and moved through the field quickly. I enjoyed the rapid course through the New Zealand farmland, delivering the 2nd fastest bike split in the age group, which was a considerable improvement on recent world champs.

Coming into transition, I could see Luce holding up four fingers, which I was chuffed to bits about, and headed out onto the run, determined to hold on to my 4th place. The run got hot and was not flat, so it quickly became a bit of a slog, but I tried to stay in the moment and not think too far ahead. I do remember coming back towards the finish, with a gleaming Lake Taupo to my left, the sun shining, and hundreds of enthusiastic supporters shouting, thinking how lucky I was, and I had to try and soak up these memories. I was fit and healthy and had the resources to fly to the other side of the world to race in a beautiful country with my family and friends.

The thoughts didn't last long as everything was hurting, and I desperately wanted to turn into the finishing chute, which was going bonkers with large crowds of very loud supporters. I think it was the best race experience I had ever had in over 20 years of competing, and finally, getting on the podium at the Ironman 70.3 World Champs with 4th place was the icing on the cake. 2024 was my most successful and enjoyable season of triathlon since I'd started. My training volume had increased again, averaging 19 hours per week, although 2-3 hours of that was mobility work, strength training, and pilates.

I've had the good fortune to have completed 132 triathlons, of which 56 have been half Ironman distance or longer. Of those 56, I've managed to get on the age group podium in 43 of them, and I've stood on the top step in 28 of them. The decision to specialise in middle-distance racing back in 2014 was a good one, and I think the consistency in results has improved over time as I've become more experienced and trained in a smarter way, and also, more latterly, had more time. I have recorded every training session I've ever done since January 2004, so I can see that over those years, I have swum 5,654 miles, ridden 132,035 miles, and run 26,521 miles. I haven't taken any of those 164,209 miles for granted and have felt particularly grateful for every mile since getting discharged from Watford General Hospital in 2017.

A week or so later, visiting a local indigenous arts and crafts school in Rotorua, I came across a Māori saying that resonated with me; *okea ururoatia,* which literally translates to *'Fight like a shark,'* or *'Strive to your utmost, be determined.'* It quite neatly summed up the last 21 years of training, racing, and competing. No matter how determined I may have been, however, any progress and success over those years was only possible by having an incredible team of people around me for either some or all of the ride.

The folks at the first club, Tri-Force, I joined in 2004, especially Simon Perkins, Dave Dawson, and Linda Pollard, were so welcoming and helpful as I started to try to find my way in the sport. I've been lucky to have come across a number of bike gurus over the years who have done a great job at keeping my bikes running smoothly, including John at Veloworx and Ryan at Lucky 13 Bikes. Simon Smart, Jamie Pringle, and Matt Bottrill have all contributed massively to my bike position, and although I still look like an inflexible old man on a bike, I can assure you that it would look far worse without their help and expertise. Keeping the body going has proved a challenge at times, although I am very grateful to Sam in the earlier years and, more latterly, to Dan at Focus Soft Tissue and Ben and Dan at Origin Health for all their time and pokey thumbs and elbows.

In terms of coaching I am very lucky to have had the pleasure of Bill Black's Wol-like wisdom for many years, together with lots of laughs. He helped me structure, prioritise and focus my training when I returned to work at Morgan Stanley in 2010, optimising my performance under some crazy time constraints. In the later years, Simon Beldon played a significant role in moving my bike performance forward at a time when I thought I was too old to be improving any further. Focusing on not just getting fitter but taking into account bike handling, pacing and riding the terrain better, and holding onto momentum, he taught me how to get faster.

However, the individual I am most grateful for is Luce. She has supported me every step of the way, not just in a passive, 'sure you can go and ride your bike' kind of way, but in a very proactive way. She is a sounding board, always there to bounce ideas off with regard to training, returning from injury, season race planning, and so many other aspects of the triathlon lifestyle.

Over the years, she has become the Queen of Logistics and

Planning, playing the key role in organising our travel, and always seems to find accommodation perfectly situated for either the swim start, transition, or the finish. She has provided comfort and invaluable advice in the darker times and has been there to celebrate the good times, always keeping me grounded. I don't take her utterly selfless support for granted; I really do know how lucky I am. Thank you.

Lesson: it is impossible to achieve your potential without the right team around you.

Epilogue

If anyone has got this far, then well done, and thanks. It has been an interesting and enjoyable exercise, and it has made me both reflect and think about what comes next. I'm only 56, after all. I am still trying to find my way in terms of figuring out retirement, finding the right balance between spending our precious time that we have worked so hard for doing things we want to do whilst also trying to find ways to give back and still play a useful role in the world. We do find the question 'yes, but what do you actually do' increasingly disconcerting and we do feel a societal-like pressure to not just do what the hell we want.

As discussed at the beginning, I'd like to write a novel, and hopefully, the prose will be of a better quality than this. With regards to triathlon, I'd love to one day win my age group at the Ironman 70.3 World Champs, although I am realistic about how hard this will be to achieve. My swimming and running are not at the required level, and I think it is now pretty much impossible to change that.

As an adult onset swimmer, I now find any gain of any sort elusive, to say the least, and I have been slowing down on the run for many years now. In the older age groups, the argument is that you just need to be the person that slows down the slowest, so there is potential to make relative gains if I'm lucky and smart, but still unlikely. So, I may just to have to wait it out for, hopefully, the 80-84 age group and hope that folks like Marcel and Cloughie have hung up their trainers.

Whilst finishing off this book, a friend of ours, Vic, very sadly died from cancer. Vic was 32 and one of those very rare people who truly lit up a room. She was kind, funny, clever, warm, positive, and just a really lovely person, who is obviously missed terribly by her husband, Jack, and her family and family-in-law, but also by many, many others. Jack and Vic quickly became part of the troop after we first met her in Pontevedra in 2019, and I will always remember her laugh and smile.

Vic died 45 days after her diagnosis, a timeline that was terrifying and shocking, especially as she was a young, healthy women who was training for the London marathon only a few weeks prior to her diagnosis. Vic showed and reminded me, the cynical introvert, that humans can be really good, and I am grateful to her for that. She has also driven home something that I was already realising; that growing old really is a privilege.

Final lesson: be more Vic